THE HAPPY BIRTHDAY BOOK OF EROTICA

Also by Alison Tyler

Best Bondage Erotica (volumes 1 and 2)
Heat Wave: Sizzling Sex Stories
Three-Way: Erotic Stories
Red Hot Erotica
Luscious
The Merry XXXmas Book of Erotica
Slave to Love
Exposed
Caught Looking (with Rachel Kramer Bussel)

THE HAPPY BIRTHDAY
BOOK OF EROTICA

EDITED BY ALISON TYLER

CLEIS
PRESS

Published in the United States by Cleis Press Inc., P.O. Box 14697, San Francisco, California 94114.

Printed in the United States.
Cover design: Scott Idleman
Cover photograph: Hugh Sitton / Getty
Text design: Frank Wiedemann
Cleis Press logo art: Juana Alicia
First Edition.
10 9 8 7 6 5 4 3 2 1

To SAM

The best birthdays of all are those that haven't arrived yet.

—ROBERT ORBEN

Let us celebrate the occasion with wine and sweet words.

—PLAUTUS

Contents

INTRODUCTION

*C*lose your eyes," he said. "*Close your eyes and make a wish—*"

When I began gathering stories for this collection, I knew exactly what I wanted: to create the most perfect birthday gift. A book filled with erotic experiences to share with a friend, lover, or that in-between sort of person you're hoping to slip up to the next step.

"*Come on, baby. Close those beautiful brown eyes for me—*"

I wanted stories of the ultimate birthday extravaganzas, tales of wanton wish fulfillment and lust. I craved experiences, the ones that would mimic or even surpass my own. The perfect birthday present doesn't involve fancy wrapping or glossy colored ribbons, unless they're tied around a lover's wrist: the definitive gift is an experience, a memory, something to savor for years to come.

"*Did you make a wish, baby doll? Don't say it out loud, or it won't come true.*"

I remember *all* of my important birthdays—and all of my

birthday sex. I turned nineteen with a leather salesman in London. He gave me a sexy sideways glance that made me want to swim the Channel for him. Or at least wait out on the steps until he got off work and we could walk the streets together, hand in hand. We found a back alley near my hotel, and when I confessed it was my birthday, he spanked me with a pair of well-worn leather gloves. To this day, whenever I smell leather, I think of him.

Twenty-one was celebrated in Hawaii, half-drunk and giddy on champagne, on a blanket on the beach. Silver moonlight and sun-warmed sand. The taste of saltwater on his skin. The gilded platinum of his hair. He kissed me all over before fucking me in the ocean, the gentle waves licking at us as he cradled me in his arms.

I was in New York for my twenty-fifth, with a raucous crowd of drag queens and so many birthday candles it seemed they lit up the night. I won four different birthday spankings—more than one hundred blows in all—and felt as if my blushing rear cheeks could have given those candles a run for the money. I was literally pink cheeked and glowing by the end of the night.

Paris at thirty: Sweet sex on a bridge as the tour boats glided below us. His firm hand in my long dark hair, tilting my head back, holding me steady as his cock slid deep inside me. We'd planned well. My full silver-gray skirt hid my front, his long black trench gave us coverage. The only people who knew what was going on were the two of us, and the old Parisian man who strolled silently by, looking over his shoulder once and giving me a wink. *"Bonsoir, mademoiselle,"* he murmured as he passed, and I felt as young and sweet as if I'd just been carded.

Everyone should turn thirty in Paris.

"A birthday spanking's what you need—"

I don't ever plan to start lying about my age. Too much

math involved on the one hand, and on the other, I'd be short-changed...on birthday spankings. Who wants to receive twenty-two swats when you can have twenty-eight? Or thirty-two? Or...?

The writers in this book all have their own ideas about what makes the perfect birthday gift. Turned on by a pair of luscious high-heeled leather boots that hug the calves? Read Shanna Germain's deliriously passionate "Puss-in-Boots."

Do you go for threesomes or foursomes, or out-of-control more-somes? You'll find them in Sage Vivant's birthday fiesta gone wild, "Forty-seven Candles," and Saskia Walker's "Party Girl on the Loose."

Ever dream of sex with a handsome stranger? Try Jolene Hui's "The Birthday Treat" or Kate Laurie's "Her Birthday Suit."

If your fantasies lean the way mine do, and you desire a delicious birthday spanking, lick your finger and turn to N. T. Morley's "More, Please, Sir," Emilie Paris's "Twenty-nine Again," or "Chasing Her Dream," by Michelle Houston, to name but three.

Now, close your eyes, make a wish, and blow out the candles.

Happy birthday, baby.

Alison Tyler
San Francisco
July 2006

HAPPY BIRTHDAY

Simone Harlow

Maris Landry unlocked the front door of her house. She shoved her keys in her purse, kicked the door shut, then slammed her purse down on the hall table. With a sigh, she unholstered her service weapon and put it on the table. Her handcuffs came next, then her detective shield. After pulling the Velcro tabs on her bulletproof vest, she yanked it over her head, and dropped it on the floor.

Happy fucking birthday to me.

She started stripping in the hall, dropping clothes as she walked to her bedroom. She needed a shower, a scotch, Cherry Garcia, and bed. In that order.

After showering and downing the single malt, she felt her day's work had earned her a ménage à trois with the most dependable men in her life, Ben and his buddy Jerry. The whole pint, no nibbling a spoonful and calling that dessert. Tonight she was licking the carton clean.

As she shoved the first delicious spoonful in her mouth, she heard the doorbell ring. It had better not be her sister, Angela, she thought, wanting to celebrate her birthday. Maris would shoot her. As she headed to the door, pulling her robe around her, the phone rang. She grabbed the cordless. "I'll be right there," she yelled at the door. "Hello?"

"Happy birthday, baby sister. How's thirty-five?"

"It sucks." She adjusted her robe. "You at the door?"

"No, but your birthday present is."

Her sister was into the S/M scene. And she often swore Maris needed to join her. "What did you get me? Leather chaps? A giant dildo? I'm sending it back."

"What did you tell me you wanted this year?"

She thought for a minute. "A twenty-year-old named Nick." Maris peeked out of the window. From her angle all she could see was a blond head. *Oh shit.* "You got me a guy?"

Angela laughed. "Not just any guy. I sent you Nick."

Maris opened the door. There in the doorway stood a blond god. Naked. Except for the big red bow hiding his stuff. "Oh my god."

"Happy birthday," Angela yelled.

Behind Naked Guy, Maris saw her neighbor's front door open a crack. She grabbed Nick's arm and pulled him inside and slammed the door. As a cop, she dealt with a lot of freaky shit, but it had never followed her home before. She was gonna cap Angela as soon as she got rid of naked Nick.

"Do you like him?"

What wasn't to like? A face like an angel, a bod built for sin. She liked him just fine. "I said young, dumb, and hung. He ain't young." She lifted his right hand. "I see a West Point ring. Class of '94. The Point means he's not dumb."

"He's younger than you."

Maris lifted up the elaborate bow. His long thick cock stood at attention like a good soldier. Her warrior cometh. "Oh my."

"One out of three ain't bad," Angela cackled.

Soldier boy Nick grinned.

She dropped the bow. "Can't you *at ease* that thing?"

Nick shrugged. "He likes you."

God help her, she was turned on. "Your name really Nick?"

He held out his hand. "Nicolas Bennett."

Maris ignored his hand. "Are you one of her...?" What was the word she called her dates?

"Her *pet*? No, I'm not a pet."

Angela laughed into the phone. "He lost a bet and he's mine for a night. I thought you needed him more than I did."

Maris was not amused. "Thanks."

"Don't mention it, Sis."

Maris gripped the phone tighter. Her sister had gone too far. "Call me next year and maybe I won't be mad at you."

"I'll see you at Mom's on Sunday. Enjoy your present."

Maris hit the disconnect button and put the phone in her robe pocket. She squared her shoulders. With her best cop face on, she took a step closer to Nick. "My pint of Ben and Jerry's is getting lonely; get your naked behind out of my house."

He crossed his arms over his massive chest. "No."

"Don't bust an attitude with me Big Dick Nick." Maris put her hands on her hips. "I'm LAPD, I'll kick your ass."

A blond eyebrow raised. "I'm ex–Special Forces. So, no... you won't."

The fact that Nick's finely rippled body was standing between her and her gun, put a new slant on the picture.

"You want me."

She did. He was a walking fuck fantasy. "You showed up.

Ha ha, big surprise. Now go." She tried to sound convincing.

"I always pay my debts."

"What did you bet on?" She couldn't keep herself from asking.

He didn't answer, at least not verbally, choosing instead to rip off the bow. Now he stood before her gloriously naked.

Maris turned her head, not wanting to stare at the package. Gawking was totally uncool. She needed to keep her pride. "Put that thing away."

He took a few steps, made a quick grab for her, and slung her over his shoulder. "Let's play." He started climbing the stairs.

"I'm not into this shit." Although this caveman routine was kinda sexy, she had to admit that, even upside down.

"We'll see."

Her stomach bounced on his shoulder all the way up the stairs. This gave her a chance to take a gander at his ass. It was high and well muscled. He had the Renoir of butts. This beat the Glock 28 her dad bought her last year.

Happy birthday to me.

Nick tossed her onto the bed. For a second she just lay there, defiance in her brown eyes. He liked that. She wouldn't be easy to tame, but she would be fun. He leaned over and slid his hand between her legs until he felt her pussy. As his fingers sunk into her moist slit, she bit her full bottom lip. Her back arched and one lush breast slipped free of her red silk robe. "Still wanna kick my ass, Detective?" he asked.

She shook her head.

He smiled, pushing his fingers further inside her. Instantly he felt her muscles clench around them. "I didn't think so." With his free hand, he untied the sash of her robe and pushed the material aside. Her high firm breasts would fit into the palms of his hands perfectly. She had a strong fit body she kept combat ready, and she clearly had fight in her. He liked that. Nick squeezed the two white globes and then bent to lick them. Maris whimpered as her legs spread wider.

"Good girl." Nick took his fingers out of her pussy. He spread her legs wider and knelt down between them. He had to taste her. He started tonguing her with broad flat strokes, licking her entire snatch. Her juices flowed. He grabbed her hips to stop her from wiggling as his tongue flicked over her hard clit. His cock grew harder as he pushed his tongue inside her as deep as it would go.

As her sweet juices met his lips, Nick suddenly couldn't stand not having his cock inside her. Lifting up her legs, he hooked them over his shoulders. Slowly he began to guide his cock into her. His instinct was to conquer and subvert, but he could tell that Maris needed a gentle hand. Anything but a straight fuck and he'd lose her.

She was so tight, at first he could only manage to get the head of his cock into her damp pussy.

"Please."

"Easy, baby, you're tight." He entered an inch at a time. The strain was destroying him; he clamored for release. Sweat beaded on his body. Using his thumb, he pulled back on the hood of her clit and began to massage her hard nub. In response, she drove her hips up and forced his cock in deeper. She began to whimper. Nick knew it was impossible for him to wait to come and he impaled her to the hilt with his straining cock. He pumped hard and fast, feeling her climaxing around him. Harder and harder he drove into her until he was ready to burst. Her tight pussy milked his cock as he exploded inside her. Nick dropped her legs and fell to his knees, laying his head gently on her stomach. He inhaled: her skin smelled like jasmine and sex.

"Happy birthday, Maris."

Maris ran her hand through his sweat-slicked hair. "You're a keeper."

Nick laughed, and it was clear from his expression that he agreed.

PARTY GIRL ON THE LOOSE

Saskia Walker

Vanessa stepped out of the hotel compound and walked up the hill without a backward glance. The Spanish resort village had everything a soul could need, but Vanessa was going stir crazy in there. She'd had quite enough lounging around, sipping *cervezas*. She'd agreed to do just that for the entire week, but it was driving her insane. Besides, there was hardly any male talent to flirt with, much to her horror. Leaving her sun-worshiping companion, Tess, to her magazines and her lounger, Vanessa announced she was bailing out for a bit of fun. Dressing in her sexiest sundress and high heels, she cracked open her hottest red lipstick and fished out her credit cards. Tess waved her off with a knowing smile, as if she'd realized all along her companion wouldn't last the distance.

Vanessa strode up the hill, feeling as if she'd broken out of jail. Adrenaline ran in her veins, her party-girl nature rising up from the ashes of a lost week lazing by the pool. "Fun," she murmured to herself, as she headed for a cluster of bars and shops. "Spanish fun is what I need." The resort wasn't in a busy area, though; it was mostly residential, but still she was hopeful. She was the kind of woman who could trigger the appropriate diversion with people who were up for it. Her theory was that fun-lovers gravitated to each other; she only had to seek out the needy.

The handful of shops proved fruitful. In the space of two hours she spent money in a designer clothes shop, a flea market, and a greengrocer, and drank cocktails in two different bars. She played blackjack with the barman in the first. In the second, she danced to gypsy guitar music on the jukebox with three sparkly-eyed grandfathers who she saw humming along to the tunes. It hadn't taken much encouragement to get them on their feet. Things were shaping up.

Alas, the grandfathers hugged her and left at siesta time. The barman told her she'd made his day. After a while she took her leave too, bereft without her party companions. She wandered on past the conglomeration of shops and bars, to where the area became more residential, with well-spaced luxury villas hidden behind hacienda-style walls.

Was that all there was? Well, she'd had some entertainment; she couldn't really complain. She was just thinking of heading back to Tess when she noticed two young men walking toward her. They were both attractive, locals it seemed to her, with dark coloring and street-smart looks. Their brand-name clothes and spiked hair were clearly meant to impress and she smiled her approval. Their pacing slowed as they looked at her with interest. When she stepped to one side of the narrow path, they stepped that way too, speaking under their breath to each other. They wanted to touch her. Sheer sexual need emanated from them. She walked straight between them, brushing against them both as she did so. The taller of the two managed to touch her breast with his arm.

Eager, oh they were eager. Lean, Latin, lover boys. Two of them. Her mouth watered. Glancing back she saw that one of them had turned around and was treading in her footsteps, a pair of sunglasses casually low so that she could see his eyes, an impish smile lifting the corners of his mouth. If he were planning to mug her, he'd have done it by now. He was up for action, and he'd picked just the woman to get a response from. Vanessa drew to a halt, one hand on her hip, watching him.

"*Hola.* Are you lost, can I help you?" The other one had disappeared. Vanessa wondered if his friend was waiting to see how he fared with her, or had he dared him to approach her?

"Is there anything to see up here?" She eyed his wiry body as she spoke. If he thought himself able to seduce an older woman, she wanted to go along with it. She leaned back casually and waved a magazine that she pulled out of one of her bags, brushing it lightly across the tops of her breasts as she fanned herself with it.

His grin spread and he adopted a relaxed pose, leaning close to her. He obviously thought his devastating charm had melted her. "I could show you around." His hands spread in an open gesture. "There is a park near here, perhaps you would like to see it?"

Vanessa reached forward and lifted his sunglasses off, looking at the sharp blue eyes that flickered with surprise when they met hers. She folded the sunglasses into the top pocket on his shirt, taking a moment to draw the back of her hand slowly across his chest, measuring him appreciatively. "And your friend?" She trailed her fingers on his collar. "Would your friend like to come too?" She raised her eyebrow at him, making sure he knew he was getting somewhere.

"Yes, Estavan will come, if you like...."

"You're trying to seduce me, aren't you?"

He grinned. "Maybe."

"How old are you?"

"Eighteen." He frowned, shaking his head. "No, nineteen."

She lifted an eyebrow again. "You're not sure?"

He laughed, a hint of a blush crossing his cheekbones. "It's my birthday today, I forgot." He shrugged.

"Birthday boy, hmm?" She had a feeling she knew what every boy's birthday dream might be. "I'll have to think of a way to help you celebrate. If you'd like."

He nodded, lips parted, pupils dilated.

This truly was like getting out of jail. She was seven years older than him, but those seven years were important ones. Was he as cool as he acted? How would he cope if she gave him a real come-on? She wanted to know. She was having fun. "And your friend, Estavan, how old is he?"

"Nineteen, he is one month older than me."

"But you are the brave one, aren't you?" She stepped closer and ran one finger along his jaw as she glanced over his fit body. Tension shot through him, his body growing taut in response to her touch. She smiled. "We'd better call Estavan back, we don't want him to feel left out now, do we?"

He shook his head, but simply stared at her.

She called down the hill. "Estavan..."

He glanced around the corner a moment later. His friend waved him up and he slinked out from his hidden spot below.

"And your name, birthday boy?" Vanessa asked.

"Jorge." His gaze followed her hand as she trailed her fingers along her cleavage. Estavan approached, looking with curiosity at his friend.

She focused her attention on him. "Jorge tells me you will show me the gardens. Are they nearby?"

After some mumbled plotting in Spanish they nodded and set off, ushering her to follow them. They spoke as they walked along. They seemed to be having some disagreement about what procedure they should adopt. Vanessa smiled to herself. They assumed she wouldn't be able to read their actions, but it was obvious they weren't sure how to proceed with their seduction of the tourist they had so bravely approached.

Inside two minutes they reached the park, deserted in the heat of the afternoon.

Once within the gates, they stood with their hands nervously pushed into their hip pockets. Vanessa glanced around. The only real cover was on the far side of the terraced lawns, by two weeping willows. She nodded over to the trees. "Shall we sit awhile in the shade? We could cool down there, perhaps?"

The lads glanced at each other and then Jorge broke into an eager smile. "Yes, let's sit there for a while." He stepped over to Vanessa's side and the two of them crossed the terrace. Estavan followed behind, glancing furtively around for passersby, like a secret agent on a mission, despite the fact that the place was deserted.

Vanessa brushed her fingers through the delicate green strands of the willow that wavered in the breeze, releasing the smell of fresh sap to her senses. The trailing willow caressed her shoulders as she ducked under the branches and entered the shaded cave beneath.

She turned to the two lads who had followed and now stood close together, just within the gloom spread beneath the tree. They stood a few paces away from her, Estavan with his hands still in his pockets. Jorge had his arms folded across his chest and glanced at her from under his dark lashes.

"What a perfect place to help Jorge celebrate his birthday."

Jorge grinned.

She dropped her bags on the ground and flexed her back. "Do you two have girlfriends?"

Estavan nodded and Jorge looked at him in surprise. "I did but she has moved to Madrid," he explained.

Vanessa nodded. Jorge didn't comment so she didn't push him. His gaze was fixed on her breasts, which she knew were rather well defined in the fitted bodice of her sundress. It was time to up the ante, to give this young man a birthday to remember. "You are looking at my breasts." Her hands closed over them. "I like that, Jorge, it makes them feel good. Like it does when I touch them." She stroked her breasts through the surface of her dress. The tension in the atmosphere heightened dramatically. Anticipation was pouring out of them. "You touch yourself, don't you, Jorge?"

The lad shifted, a guilty smile twitching at the corners of his mouth.

"It's okay. Everybody does it. It's a beautiful thing, to make yourself come. You shouldn't be ashamed." They were hanging on her every word, astonished and enthralled. "If you can't love your own body, you can't love the body of another...." She trailed her hand around the back of her neck. The two of them looked as taut as arrows about to spring from a bow. She gave a low chuckle and leaned her back up against the tree trunk.

"Estavan, do you like to pleasure yourself?"

"Pleasure...?"

"Masturbate, wank, jerk off?"

"*Masturbarse*," Jorge translated.

After a moment's hesitation, Estavan nodded.

"Do you do it often?" She smoothed the skirt of her dress down over her hips. "Confess!" she demanded, with a naughty smile.

"I do it every day," Jorge interrupted, in a low voice, drawing her attention back to him. "Why do you want to know?" The restraint in his voice was equal to the tension in his body. Vanessa could see the bulge in his jeans. She eyed it openly.

"It makes me hot, to think of you doing it," she whispered. "It makes me hot here." Her hand closed over her pubic bone, her fingers pushing the material of her dress between her thighs. She wasn't wearing underwear, so she knew they would see where the fabric dipped into her groin. "I'm burning up thinking about you wanking. Tell me about it." Her hand moved back and forth. "If you tell me, I'll show you just how hot it makes me."

"I have to do it," Jorge said, his gaze riveted on her moving hand. "Or I will go mad."

Vanessa began to slide her skirt up, swishing the material slowly across her thighs. He groaned as he caught sight of her naked pubic hair. She rested the material of her skirt around her waist, capturing it with her elbows, and then slid her hands over her hip bones. "Would you like to see me pleasure myself, Jorge? I would like to see you doing it. Show me."

He was riveted, his jeans bulging, but apparently he was still in need of more encouragement.

"You know you want to show me, Jorge, and I want to see it." Her finger opened up the folds of her sex, squeezing her swollen clit, her legs spreading as she leaned back into the tree.

His eyes were frantic, the lust was there and it was only inexperience holding him back from leaping on her.

"Would you go mad, if you couldn't pleasure yourself, right now?"

His face was flushed, his eyes dark as cobalt as he stared at her bare pussy. "Yes, yes." He fumbled with his jeans, his mouth open. He was panting with anticipation. His eyes flashed shut briefly when his hand closed over his erect cock.

Powerful in her sexuality, her thrill was multiplied by the effect she was having on them. Her fingers moved languorously over her clit and through the slick, wet folds of her sex as she watched him. "Beautiful, your cock is very beautiful, Jorge."

Jorge staggered nearer her, his fist working faster and faster on his proud cock. "Please..." He licked his lips, his eyes pleading.

He was so polite! It tweaked something inside her to hear his urgent plea. "Go on then, taste me."

He fell to his knees, his face pressing urgently into her pussy. She felt his tongue whip along her fingers and dip between the folds of her sex. He mouthed hungrily at her, tasting what he quite obviously longed to have a go at. He gave a tantalizing flick at her clitoris, then his head went back and she felt the spray of his ejaculation fly up her leg.

His brief moves brought her heady, raw pleasure; her groin was suffused with heat and sensation. She was hot for more, really hot. She looked at Estavan. He had stood, motionless, his face dark with envy and desire as he observed his friend. "Come closer if you want to."

Jorge rested back on his knees, his cock still hard in his hand as he watched. Estavan stepped forward. She took his arm and drew his fingers to her sex. "Does it feel good?" she asked, rubbing his hand there.

"Yes," Estavan replied, through gritted teeth.

Jorge reached forward and pushed her dress higher on her hips, freeing her hands. She began to rotate her hips on Estavan's fingers, her body pivoting against the tree trunk. His face was contorted with lust; he pressed closer against her, pushing her back against the tree.

"You want me inside you, don't you?" he blurted. "I can do it." The lust in his eyes, his containment, his nerve, thrilled Vanessa.

"Lie down," she commanded, and pushed him down on the grass. Jorge was still kneeling on the ground, watching, his cheeks flushed.

When Estavan lay back, Vanessa ripped open his jeans. The swollen head of his cock bobbed out, hard and ready. She gave a delighted laugh, intoxicated by the moment, and climbed over him. When she sank onto his cock, he groaned loudly. She ground hard onto him, circling quickly, leaning over him as sensation mounted. "Oh yes," she moaned when waves of heat throbbed up through her.

Estavan looked at her with fascination, his cock stiff and his body taut, lifting up from the ground.

She rose up and plunged again. "Do you like it?"

"Harder, harder," he replied, nodding, his face contorted. She flexed her hips and rode him faster. His hands clutched at the grass either side of his body; he was helpless beneath her. She could feel his release mounting up inside her and ground close against him, his balls riding up against her buttocks. His hips were wriggling now; he could not come quickly enough. He was in pain with it.

She leaned back, bowing his cock inside her, powering the release. "Your prick is magnificent, Estavan," she said. "It's so hard it's making me gush inside." With that, he exploded, his cries of anguish rising up through the branches of the tree.

Vanessa was still hot for more. She hadn't come yet. She climbed off, rolled onto her back and touched herself. Her clit was throbbing. She circled it, her fingers focusing the sensation. The pungent smell of sex floated in the warm air, dancing with the scent of sap from the trees. She was intoxicated. Her knees drew up, her thighs falling open.

Her eyes opened to see the tapestry of willow green moving with the flecks of brilliant blue sky above her. Then she felt a tentative touch on her thighs and, glancing down, she saw Jorge was there, ready to take her to her peak. He kneeled over her, watching her fingers move, his erection standing proud as ever, and his hips pressing forward for her appraisal. It was a beautiful thing, his sturdy prick. So hard and ready for her again.

"Hello, birthday boy," she whispered. "What did you get for your birthday?"

His eyes flashed with amusement. "You."

She nodded. "Official party girl, that's me."

His hand was on his cock, stroking it.

"I hope you enjoy your present." She winked. "Come on then," she whispered, and reached out her arm to him.

He muttered to himself in Spanish and fell on her. She growled when his cock jabbed at her tender, swollen clitoris and then she guided him to the right place, her legs closing around him as he sank into her with a moan of contentment. His face fell against her neck, his mouth pecking hungrily at her skin as his hips began to thrust furiously. He rose up on his arms, looking down at her with longing, as if amazed at the effect he was having on her. His increasingly violent thrusts were so quick and keen she was building and building with them, her sex flooded with heat.

"It's so good!" She moaned with pleasure, looking into his eyes and letting him know what he was giving her, her hips arched to take him in. "I'm going to come, Jorge, you are making me come." Loud, wet slurping sounded every time he thrust in and out, she was so wet. Weight gathered, her clit was thrumming, her sex clutching at him over and over as she climaxed.

"Fuck, fuck," he shouted and she felt the quick succession of thrusts, heard the repeated cursing as he climaxed, his body suddenly jerking out of control. His cock slid out and semen pumped over the grass. He gave a deep guttural moan as his body spasmed and shuddered, his arms trembling violently. He collapsed over her.

Vanessa stroked his head, a smile hovering on her mouth.

"Can I kiss you?" It was Estavan, leaning over and looking down at her. The shy one had turned out to be the bravest, after all. He'd asked for the first fuck.

She crooked her finger and slid her hand around his neck as he descended to touch his lips against hers. As she teased his tongue into her mouth with hers, she felt Jorge stirring against her neck and his teeth nibbling at her throat. He murmured something in Spanish. Estavan pulled back and chuckled.

"What did he say?"

Jorge lifted his head. "I said you're the best birthday present I ever had, party girl."

"Good."

"It's my birthday tomorrow," Estavan said, grinning.

Vanessa laughed, heady with pleasure. "I bet it is." She winked at Jorge, who had told her Estavan was a month older.

"It is, really."

She sighed with pleasure, stretching languorously on the grass. *My work here is not yet done,* she thought to herself, with a chuckle. "In that case, it's just as well party girl isn't flying home until the day after."

The two of them cheered and exchanged a high five over her. Just like she had always said, fun-lovers always gravitated to each other.

MORE, PLEASE, SIR

N. T. Morley

Gina shifted nervously from side to side. The room was full of people, and they were all looking at her. It was, after all, her birthday.

And she was naked, having stripped off her skirt and blouse just a moment ago.

"You get to choose," Ronald told her.

"Choose—" she stammered, trying her best not to cover herself up with her hands.

"Choose who you would like to spank you first."

She knew she was being punished, after a fashion. She had frustrated her Master with her love of being spanked. He had put her across his knee many times, her ass tilted just so and her naked body wriggling with each stroke he gave her. Her pussy got wet from the first blow every time, but no matter how long he spanked her, no matter how red and hot and aching her ass was after ten or twenty or thirty minutes of punishment, she always said the same thing.

"More, please, Sir."

It might have been her submissive nature; after all, she had been trained to accept whatever happened to her, to beg for more. But with spanking, Ronald had instructed her that he would spank her until she begged him to stop—or until he had reached the limits of his endurance.

She had never begged him to stop. And that's why Gina stood, now, nude in their living room with three people looking at her—two men, one woman. All three had cruel smiles on their faces.

Where should she start? There was Jess, a friend of Ronald's who had spanked her once before at a party. His wife, Monica, was a woman Gina particularly liked. Then there was Charles, an older man who frightened her a bit with the hungry way he looked at her. Though he had never spanked her, she had once seen him minister to a pert bottom at the same party where Gina had been spanked by Jess—and it had been quite a sight, even amazing a dedicated spanking bottom like Gina with its intensity.

"I'd like to start with Monica, Sir," said Gina.

"Then go ahead," Ronald told her. "Let the spankings begin."

Gina nervously walked over to the couch and lay down across both Monica's and Jess's laps, her face buried in the cushions. She gasped slightly as she felt Monica's hand rest on her bottom, then travel down between her thighs. Monica took a moment to tease Gina's pussy a little, while Gina squirmed in her grasp and whimpered. Jess's fingertips traced a path up her calves as Monica drew her hand back.

The first blow made Gina yelp. She pushed her ass in the air as Monica's hand rose and fell, the flat of her palm bringing slapping sounds. Gina's ass warmed quickly and Monica struck her harder. Gina's pussy flooded as the spanking intensified, and soon she was moaning. She opened her mouth wide and bit the couch cushion hard. She lifted her ass higher and met Monica's blows eagerly.

"You like that?" asked Monica as Gina pushed up against her.

"More, please," said Gina. "More, please, Ma'am."

Monica complied, spanking faster and harder while Jess stroked Gina's inner thighs. Monica paused so Jess could slide two fingers inside Gina; her cunt was molten and she moaned loudly. Jess withdrew and Monica began to spank her again, clearly excited by the ritual. Before long, however, Monica was winded.

"Finished yet?" she asked.

"More, please," said Gina, pitifully. "More."

"Jess, it's your turn," said Monica.

Gina squirmed her way down the sofa until she rested firmly over Jess's lap, the way she had when he'd spanked her before. She could feel his cock, quite hard against her belly, and the feeling excited her. Her pussy responded with a tightness that coaxed her deeper into submission.

Now Gina's face was in Monica's lap, and she could smell the sharp scent of Monica's pussy from under the short dress she wore. Monica ran her hands through Gina's hair and stroked her back as Jess began to spank her.

Jess spanked her harder than Monica had, building a rhythm as Gina whimpered and moaned. When he paused to finger her cunt again after a few minutes, a drizzle of juice ran down Gina's thigh. Monica reached down and teased Gina's clit, which had grown swollen and firm with arousal.

"She's very wet," Monica announced. "Does she come from spanking?"

"Not at all," said Ronald. "Perhaps that's why she keeps asking for more."

"No," said Monica, withdrawing her hand. "I think she's just a little spanking slut. Hit her harder, Jess."

Jess's strokes grew in intensity as Gina's pert cheeks grew pinker. He moved from her ass to the backs of her thighs, which were much more sensitive. He struck them lightly at first, then harder. Gina only pushed up against him and moaned. Her ass turned a deep red; there would be bruising later, and Gina knew she would finger every bruise with pleasure.

"Had enough?" Jess asked her, his voice resonant with arousal.

"More, please, Sir," said Gina. "More, please."

Monica seized Gina's hair, pulled her to her hands and knees, raising her ass high in the air. Gina felt the most naked she had all evening. Then Monica kissed Gina, her tongue exploring Gina's mouth as Gina obediently parted her lips.

"Charles is next," said Ronald. Gina crawled off of the couch and went to the loveseat where Charles sat. She was just small enough to tuck herself into it with her ass pushed up high.

Charles, too, was hard, but she tilted her body at just the angle that prevented too much contact with his cock. Charles responded by pushing her down, grinding her belly against his cock through his slacks. He chuckled.

"You want more, do you?" he growled.

"Yes," said Gina. "More, please, Sir."

Charles spanked her even harder than Jess had, bringing an instant cry from Gina's lips. She had been right to fear him; he was cruel in the way he spanked her. Gina thrashed in Charles's lap, clutching the arm of the loveseat and gasping loudly with each hard blow. Gina felt her ass catching fire with the stinging sensation; she had never been spanked for this long before.

As Gina's ass flushed deeper, now an angry red, Charles switched from open-handed blows to the side of his hand, rapping Gina hard, hitting her sweet spot firmly at its thickest point. There would be deep bruising from that, she knew, deeper than the bruises from Monica's or Jess's blows. Or the blows Ronald gave her every night when he spanked her. Gina's ass was hot, pulsing and throbbing with every blow, sensitized to every touch.

Charles switched back to an open hand, spanking Gina in a smooth rhythm for what seemed like an eternity. Gina sank into the feeling, her heart pounding as she took more than she had ever taken.

Charles did not ask her if she had had enough; on the contrary, he seemed to be spanking her purely for his own enjoyment. When she let out a particularly loud moan or whimper of distress, he would chuckle. He didn't pause to finger her pussy, either, but she could feel the hard blows of his hand making her clit pulse with the impact.

It felt like she was going to come.

There was something about the way Charles spanked her, something about the rhythm he used, that conjured a powerful heat not just in her ass but in her clitoris as well. She seethed and pitched against him, pumping her hips rapidly. And still he spanked her, without pausing to see if she was enjoying it. She felt helpless over his lap in a way she never had with Ronald, always knowing he would stop when she begged him to.

With Charles, she wasn't so sure.

The sensation mounted; the pain grew as Charles hit her still harder. She was reaching her limit, and everyone in the room knew it.

Gina cried out, louder than she had yet—and choked back what sounded like a sob. She was right on the edge of a climax, an experience she had never had before—coming from a spanking.

"Had enough?" asked Charles.

The word formed in her mouth, but she could only get out a

tortured "Mmmmm" sound before she stopped, swallowed, and gasped. "I've had enough, Sir," she said. "Thank you."

"Then come over here and get some more," she heard Ronald's voice. He had taken his place in an armchair opposite Charles. Gina felt a wave of fear; she was so close to coming, but she had asked them to stop. And now Ronald was going to spank her some more. She quivered as she rose and walked over to her Master's chair.

"Over my knee," said Ronald.

Gina took her place, her pained ass pushed up high.

She gritted her teeth as she felt her Master's hand stroking its way up her inner thigh. She awaited his first blow, shutting her eyes tightly.

Instead, she felt him parting her lips with his hand, then sliding two fingers deep inside her. His thumb struck her clit, and as he began to finger her, she came.

Gina came harder than she had ever come before. She clawed at the arm of the chair, shuddering and squirming across Ronald's lap. Her moans filled the room, and approving sounds came from Monica and Jess and Charles. Ronald kept fingering Gina as her orgasm intensified; he could feel the clenching muscles of her pussy as she came. When she was finished, she let out a long, low wail of release.

Ronald slid his fingers out of her and pressed gently on her reddened cheeks.

Gina felt hungry, her pussy opened. The sting of her ass as Ronald touched her there made her pussy clench tighter.

"Now," said Ronald, "I think you've had enough."

Gina felt her lips moving, heard the whimper deep in her throat.

"What was that?" asked Ronald.

Gina cleared her throat. She took a deep breath.

"More, please," she said softly. "More, please, Sir."

Ronald drew back his arm with a gleeful laugh, and Gina whimpered in anticipation of the next stroke.

PUSS-IN-BOOTS

Shanna Germain

I found them by accident. I'd given up the search, days, maybe a week ago even. Then, the night before his birthday, there they were, in the window of a secondhand store: the boots. Knee-high, black leather with at least a five-inch heel. Even through the window glass, I could tell the leather was that soft, stretchy kind, something with enough give to slide over my muscled calves. I leaned in closer to the window, put one hand up to block out the glare from the streetlamp. The toes were long, but not pointed. Jesus, they were perfect, just what my husband had asked for. I'd been so sure I wasn't going to find these boots that I'd already bought him an expensive backup gift. Who cared? I'd been given a last-minute blessing and I wasn't about to turn it away.

When I exhaled, my breath fogged up the glass, and I realized I'd been leaning in so close my nose was almost against the window. I wanted to wipe away the fog, keep my eyes on the boots.

I had a sudden fear that someone was already inside, getting ready to buy them. Or that I would walk in and the salesperson would say, "Sorry, only for show," and then I would have to get down on my hands and knees and beg her, offer her anything, anything, for those boots. Maybe she'd just let me borrow them for the night.

The door didn't open at first, and there was a fresh fear that I hadn't thought of, that they'd be closed already, that I would spend the night kicking myself for leaving work too late. But then I pushed instead of pulled and the door swung open to the smell of incense and patchouli and the insides of old purses.

The dark-haired girl behind the counter gave me a half smile, just the corners of her lips curling up. Normally, she was the kind of girl I would have stayed and flirted with—cute in an almost boyish way, funny, great smile. But I had other things on my mind.

"Those boots," I blurted, pointing to the window. "Are they for sale?"

The girl smiled again, this time for real, showing off small, perfectly straight teeth.

"Everything's for sale," she said. "Well, except for me." She paused, seemed to think about her answer. "Well, at least not usually."

Something flooded through my stomach. "Thank god," I said. "I'll take them."

She hesitated, tucked a dark curl behind her ear. "Don't you want to know how much? Or the size or anything?"

I shook my head. It didn't matter. If they were size six, I'd pop a couple of aspirin ahead of time and squeeze my feet into them for a couple of hours. Even if they cost a hundred dollars, I didn't care. I'd put it on my card. My husband was only going to turn thirty once.

She took the black boots from the window display, put them on the counter. I resisted the urge to stroke the length of the leather.

"Twenty-two bucks," she said. "Size eight."

I had to laugh. It was too good to be true. They were a little big—I wear seven and a half—but I couldn't have asked for more. I wanted to hug the girl behind the counter, but she was already looking at me like I was kind of nuts, so I just put my card on the glass and said "Thank you."

"My pleasure, apparently." She put two fingers on the long, thin heel of a boot, stroked it gently. "Or maybe someone else's?"

I blushed then. So obvious. She could have overcharged me by a hundred bucks and I still would have said yes, I was that desperate.

Then she wrapped the boots in tissue paper, slowly and carefully, without looking at me, and put them in a bag. "You come back and let me know how it turns out, okay?"

"Okay," I promised—she really was cute, with that smile— and then I took my boots home to plan.

That night, I couldn't sleep. I'd put the boots in the back of the closet, next to our toys, and the thought of them nestled there, waiting, was almost more than I could stand. I wanted to slide them on now, wake him up with one heel pressed to his thigh. But I didn't. I just watched him sleep—the little laugh lines around his eyes that were new this year, the gray hairs at his temple—and imagined what I would wear with the boots tomorrow: my wraparound dress with nothing under it, a long button-up shirt half-buttoned, or nothing but a black thong and a silver necklace....

In the end, I chose the black wraparound dress, nothing

under it but me. I slid it on before he got home, tied it loosely around my waist. Then I pulled the boots up over my ankles and calves. The leather curved perfectly around my calves and stopped just below the knee. I could barely walk in the heels, but I figured it didn't matter: if I could just knock his eyes out when he walked in the door, I'd be okay. I tied my long hair up in a sexy, kind of librarian bun. Then I sat down on the bed and waited.

It wasn't long before I heard the fumble of keys as he came through the front door. "Hon?" he called.

I stood up, brushed down the back of my dress, and leaned against the wall with what I hoped was a sexy, come-hither look and not a these-heels-are-too-high look. "In here," I said.

He came in, head down, hands focused on undoing his tie. "What's the deal with—" He lifted up his head and saw me.

"Happy birthday," I said, quickly. Standing there with nothing on but boots and a dress so thin you could see the points of my nipples through it, I was nervous. What had I been thinking? Surely he'd been kidding when he'd asked me to buy him boots for his thirtieth birthday. Jesus, I was nearly thirty myself, too old for knee-high boots and this sexy pose I was trying to pull off. My fingers tightened on the tie of my dress.

"Jesus," he said. His voice was breathy, like he'd been hit in the gut. For some reason, that made me feel a little better, like maybe this hadn't been such a bad idea. And then I saw his eyes, the way they were even darker than usual, and a shiver went through me. Yes, this was what he'd been asking for.

Those dark eyes were silent on me so long that my thighs broke out in goose bumps all the way up to my cunt. The combination of nerves and excitement had me shivering. I was afraid my teeth would chatter if he waited any longer. I inhaled, swallowed.

"Well, unwrap me already," I said, and then I had to laugh at the nervous impatience in my voice.

He didn't seem to notice, or care. He just came close enough that I could see the cat's-whisker wrinkles at the corners of his eyes. His hands on my lower back were warm and strong. After he pulled me against him, he ran his hands down around the curves of my ass, saying, "Oops," the same way he used to fake yawn and put his arm around me in movie theaters. Hands settled into the curve at the bottom of my ass, he put his mouth to my earlobe and gave it a tug with his teeth.

"What if I don't want to unwrap you?" he asked.

There were those goose bumps again, everywhere on my body, like they were inside too. I leaned against him, and the warmth of his chest calmed my skin, the press of his already-hard cock lit my skin on fire once more. I swallowed, trying to gain some sort of control. I'd forgotten how sexy he could be when he was turned on.

"Well, if you don't unwrap me, then you can't have your present," I said.

He just held me away from him, both arms straight out and me on the ends of his hands, like I was a painting he'd just found.

"Jesus," he said. "You just look gorgeous. Those boots..."

He dropped his head, and I looked where he was looking: down at the boots rising up my calves, the contrast between the black leather and the pale skin.

"You really like them?" I asked.

In answer, he went down on his knees in front of me. I gave a second of thought to his poor knees on the wood floor, thought about reminding him that he wasn't as young as he was yesterday, but then he put his mouth right at the edge of the boot, right where the leather met my skin. He licked it, the half leather, half skin, and I felt his warm tongue and the slight scrape of teeth around the side of my calf. My goose bumps came back, peppering all the way up my legs and back. Beneath the thin fabric of the dress, my nipples tightened. The only thing I could say was, "Oh."

He ran his hand up one boot, then the other, his palms sliding over each ankle and shin and calf. I've never been much of a foot person—I find hips and chests and cocks and smiles sexier than feet—but there was something about the way he caressed my skin through the leather that made me understand why people found it a turn-on.

Then he went back to kissing the skin right along the edge of the boots, right in the hollow at the back of my knee. With each kiss, he slid his hand a little farther up my thigh. When he reached my cunt, his fingers slid against it, then in, easily. "You're so wet," he said. He put his mouth to my belly, wiggled the ends of his fingers inside me until I shivered. "Thought this was supposed to be *my* birthday present."

"Sorry," I said. But the way he said it, I knew he didn't mind that I was enjoying it as much as he was.

When he came up from his kneeling position, he slipped his fingers out and his cock inside me. He was fully hard, and felt longer than usual—maybe it was the angle—and I moaned in surprise and pleasure as he made his way up. He thrust inside me, kissing my chin, my cheeks, the side of my nose, somewhere new with each movement of his hips. In my boots, I was almost as tall as he was—I didn't have to stand on my tiptoes to meet him, I was lifted up, with him balancing me on his cock.

He slid out of me. "Let's get on the bed," he said. "I can't see your boots from here."

He undressed fast, a kid with a present in front of him, unable to slow down. Then, he climbed on the bed and lay down on his back with his hands behind his head. I almost laughed: lying that way, he was all cock; the way it stuck up away from his body, that sweet curve toward his belly that I loved.

I reached down, started to peel the boots down.

"No, please," he said. "Leave them on."

"What about the bedspread?"

"Do I look like I care?" he asked.

And gazing at him lying there naked, cock up and waiting for me, I realized that I didn't care either. I climbed onto the bed and straddled him, keeping the boots as close to his hips as I could, so he would feel the leather every time I moved. I found his cock with my hand, and squatted over him, my thighs already starting to ache. But I didn't care, it was worth it to feel him inside me like this.

I slid myself slowly down over his cock, taking him in little bit by little bit, loving the way his eyes closed and his mouth opened. He didn't make much of a sound until I grabbed his shoulders and used the leverage to lift myself up and down on his cock. Then he moaned, his head back a little, and reached out and grabbed the boots at the ankles. The feel of his hands through the leather made my cunt ache like it was empty even though he was already inside me.

"Want to switch?" he asked after a few minutes. And I did, but I didn't. My thighs burned from holding myself over him, but everything else was burning too, in a good way. Then I remembered: This was his birthday. Not mine.

"Do you?" I asked. He pumped his hips up into me a few times, hard and quick, his eyes closed.

"Let's switch," he said. "I need a condom anyway."

While he grabbed one from the dresser, I rolled over on the bed so that when he turned back around, I was all ass and boots. He didn't even stop to put the condom on—just put his hands around the sides of my ass and slid himself back into me.

"Jesus," he said. "You're killing me."

"Well, you're old enough now to have life insurance, so maybe I am," I said.

Instead of responding, he thrust into me harder, which is what I knew he'd do. I leaned back into his thrusts. I love that position, the way his balls slap against me, the way he reaches around, like he was doing now, to find my nipples, tweak them.

"Bitch," he said, and dropped his hand off my nipple and put his finger right on my clit.

"Shit." My voice was mostly breath and push, then the sharp inhale of pleasure.

After a second, he dropped his finger away and pulled out of me. I moaned, aching from lack. I heard the sound of the condom wrapper, and felt him pushing back into me, different now, but just as hard, just as much him.

And then he wrapped his hands around the ankles of the boots, lifted them up. For a second, it was like a new yoga pose—doggie-style with boots. But then my hips settled in, and I could push back into him. His hands tightened around my ankles with each thrust.

"You're going to have to get yourself off," he said. At first I didn't understand, but then I realized he meant because his hands were full. I went down on one shoulder, pushing my ass even further in the air, and reached down with one hand. My clit was huge and wet, and as soon as I touched it, it sent shivers through me. I felt kind of bad, because it was his birthday, and I was the one getting myself off.

But then he said, "Go ahead," and I realized it was good for him too, feeling me finger myself while he was inside me. I rubbed my clit hard while he fucked me; thought about him behind me, his hands tight around my ankles. I came before he did, but it was okay, because when he came, he came a long time, shuddering into me, dropping the boots and leaning over my back like he couldn't hold himself up. His heart was pounding against my back, matching the pumping of my own heart and clit.

"Jesus," he said against my back. "Jesus, Jesus."

I laughed, and gave him a bit of shove so he'd start moving. He did, and I rolled over and pulled off the boots. He watched me from the bed, his cock still wrapped in the condom.

"I'm not even going to ask where you found those boots," he said.

I lay down beside him, our bodies only warmth and skin and sweat.

"I had to trade my soul for them."

He snuggled up to my neck.

"Hmm," he said. "It was well worth it."

"I hope so," I said. "Happy birthday, baby."

When he laughed, I saw the new lines around his mouth too, little smile echoes.

"Yes, it is." Then he sighed. "This morning I felt old."

"And now?"

"Now, not so much."

"Good," I said.

"Plus," he said, putting his hands in my hair, and kissing my chin, "you're catching up. Next month, you'll be as old as me. And I have no idea what you're going to ask for, but I highly doubt you can top those boots."

I rolled over and moved closer to him, so I could feel his heartbeat against my back again. I thought of the girl behind the counter, her short dark hair and playful eyes, the way she'd smiled when she'd wrapped up the boots. "Oh, I'm sure I'll think of something," I said.

THE BIRTHDAY PARTY

Marilyn Jaye Lewis

I opened my eyes in the middle of the night and at first I thought I was dreaming.

Danny was there, standing next to the bed, shaking me gently.

"Get up, Louanne, I have a surprise for you," he was saying.

"What's going on, Danny? What time is it?"

"It doesn't matter what time it is. I have a surprise for you."

That's when I realized that we weren't alone, that there was someone else in the dark there with us. "Who's here, Danny? What's going on?"

"Relax. It's that guy from the bar, remember?"

I remembered all right, but I wasn't sure I'd been serious.

"You've got to be kidding, Danny."

"Don't tell me you've changed your mind. He's totally into it, Louanne, and he doesn't even want the money."

"I'm more than happy to do it for free, honey. For a pretty girl like you."

I couldn't believe I was hearing it, that voice coming at me in the darkness. It was really happening. All that stood between me and my dream lover was my mouth saying that I refused to go through with it.

"Don't be scared, Louanne," the voice continued. "I know exactly what you want. Danny told me all the details, right down to keeping the lights off."

I pulled the blankets around myself protectively and listened to my heart pound.

"Danny," I said quietly, barely able to get the words out. "I don't know."

"I'll be right here," he assured me. "It'll be perfect, the best birthday gift you could want."

"All right," I heard myself saying, "all right."

"Do you have the outfit? Can you find it in the dark?"

"I think I can."

"Do you want us to leave you alone while you get dressed?"

"No, Danny. Stay here. I'm afraid of changing my mind."

The room grew incredibly quiet as I got out of bed and felt my way through the closet and dresser drawers in the dark. All I could hear was the two of them breathing.

I felt a little awkward dressing like that, as if I were overdoing it. A black velvet gown and high heels, my best pearls—in the pitch darkness. Knowing full well what was coming, I wasn't sure I could really go through with it; I felt too vulnerable. Still, I had to admit I was excited at the same time.

"I'm ready, Danny," I said at last, "but swear to me you'll keep the lights off."

"I swear, Louanne. I'll keep the lights off."

I sat down in the chair by the window, raised the blinds so the dim moonlight could filter in. I smoothed down my full skirt and waited.

It seemed like an eternity that I sat there with my heart pounding.

"Hey, birthday girl," he finally said. "You look really pretty in the moonlight."

His hips were planted firmly in front of my face. I was afraid to look up at him for fear that I might see him too clearly and have a change of heart.

"Thank you," I said softly.

He knelt down in front of me then and carefully removed my high heels.

"These seem awfully pretty," he said. "Probably expensive, huh?"

"A little," I replied.

His hands were warm as they slipped under my long skirt and then felt for the tops of my stockings. His fingers brushing against the skin of my upper thighs aroused me and I couldn't help but part my legs for him. The crinoline lining of my dress rustled against him as he lowered first one of my stockings and then the other, sliding them off me completely.

Then he reached around me and put my hands behind my back, using one of the stockings to tie my wrists together. With him on his knees, his face close to mine, I could feel his breath on my face and he appealed to me. When he finished tying me, he kissed my mouth, pushing his tongue in, and as he kissed me, he pulled down the front of my strapless gown and exposed my breasts.

He kissed me for a long time, his tongue filling my mouth while his hands squeezed my tits and tugged my nipples. Then he collected himself.

He stood and had me scoot off the chair. "Get on your knees," he said.

Danny lit a cigarette suddenly and the match seemed blinding.

"Danny!" I cried, startled.

"Sorry," he said urgently. "I'm sorry. Keep going, Louanne."

But the sudden burst of flame in the dark had unsettled me. It had lasted just long enough for me to catch a good look at myself on my knees, my most expensive dress tugged down and my tits exposed. But thankfully the darkness returned before I'd had a chance to see the face of the guy looking down at me. That might have been enough to make me change my mind altogether.

Instead we kept going.

The man unzipped his jeans and his erection sprang out full and hard. He grabbed my hair and guided my face to his cock. It felt warm.

"Go on," he said. "Kiss it all over."

I did as I was told, almost overcome with lust. I pretended that I didn't have a choice, that this good-looking stranger from the bar who was holding my hair had overpowered me.

"That's good, that's right," he said. "Now lick it. I want to feel your tongue. Go all the way down to my balls. That's right, birthday girl, lick them good. Now come back up and lick the head."

I couldn't believe he was playing his part so perfectly. As he held tight to my hair he said, "Take it now, suck my dick." Then he drove his cock in and out of my mouth. I tried to keep my balance but I was unsteady on my knees, my hands too securely tied behind my back. Once or twice it seemed the only thing keeping me upright was his grip on my hair. My jaw was starting to ache. He was pumping into me relentlessly; spit was collecting in my mouth because he wasn't giving me a chance to swallow.

Finally, he helped me up and led me over to the bed where Danny was sitting. The man tossed me facedown onto it, but he was more playful than rough. Right away his hands were under my skirt, tugging down my panties.

I was so wet that when my panties came down I felt unusually exposed.

When they were off completely, he wedged some pillows under me to raise my ass in the air. He shoved my dress up high. I could feel the rough hem against my bare shoulders. Then he spread my thighs wide.

"Oh god," I moaned softly when I felt him touch me.

"Birthday girl, you are so wet. You must be having a really good time."

His fingers spread my swollen lips apart and his tongue darted all over my stiff clit. He licked me thoroughly, until he was burrowing his tongue deep into my hole.

It was then that Danny knelt in front of me on the bed and undid his jeans. He took his erection out and slid it into my mouth, making me arch my neck uncomfortably.

I sucked him eagerly, though, while the other guy kept licking my dripping pussy; he pressed his face flush against me and jammed his tongue into my hole, his hands keeping me spread wide. I could tell it had been a while since he'd shaved, but the friction felt good on my engorged lips. When he started to groan, I squirmed hard against his face.

"Oh, Louanne," Danny was saying as he worked his dick in and out of my mouth, "you look so pretty like this, so hot; spread out and wiggling your little ass. You look like you want to get fucked, you know that? You want to get fucked, Louanne? You want a hard dick in your hot little hole?"

I was moaning eagerly in agreement while I sucked Danny's cock, but my hands were still tied behind me and I had no other choice. I had to go at the pace they chose.

"He looks to me like he might be ready," Danny taunted me. "You want to get fucked now, Louanne? You want to get fucked really hard? What do you say, birthday girl?"

At last, Danny took his cock from my mouth so that I could speak.

"Yes," I said. "I do. I want to get fucked really hard, Danny."

I felt the guy get off the bed. I heard him get undressed. In an instant he was back, his knees were between my thighs and he had a tight grip on my ankles.

Then he pushed his dick into my waiting hole. He was substantially endowed. The full length of his cock going into my vagina made me cry out.

He pumped into me hard and deep, and all I could do was lie there, my ass propped up on the pillows for him, my ankles pinned to the bed.

Danny was back at my mouth, going at me in a brisk rhythm. I knew he was almost ready to come.

"Jesus," he was chanting, clutching my hair. "Jesus, Louanne."

I was whimpering and carrying on from the force of the cock thrusting into me from behind. Danny jerked against my face hard and started to come down my throat. I felt like I was going to choke.

When Danny had finished coming, he scooted aside and watched me get nailed in the moonlight.

I really started to sputter and cry then. The harder and deeper the guy fucked me, the better it felt.

"Oh," I was crying, "oh god." I realized I was actually coming then and he wasn't ready to let up on me. He pounded away at me until my spread legs ached.

When he finally did come, I felt suddenly shy again. Everyone was coming down to earth quickly and I realized I didn't even know the guy's name.

"That was really fun," he said while he started to put on his clothes. But when he moved to untie my hands, Danny intervened.

"Don't," he said. "Leave them tied just a little longer."

"Why?" I wanted to know. "What's going on?"

"It's well after midnight," Danny explained. "We're deep into the birthday zone."

"Danny, no," I protested, knowing him too well.

"Come on now, be a good girl."

"Danny, no, I mean it."

But Danny ignored my halfhearted plea and told the guy to sit back down on the bed.

"She's already wearing her birthday dress," Danny explained to him. "It's a shame not to let her have her birthday spankings, too."

The guy seemed more than delighted to oblige Danny. He shifted me over his knee and raised my skirt once more while I struggled lamely to squirm away. "Come on," he said, slapping my naked ass, "you're a big girl. You can take it, Louanne. A spank for each year. It'll be over before you know it."

"That's what you think," Danny laughed as he leaned against the headboard and relaxed in the dark. "Wait'll you hear how old she is."

OPTIONS

Jacqueline Sinclaire

Happy birthday to you…"

Her voice was low and sultry in my ear and I wondered when she would relieve me of this blindfold.

"Happy birthday to you!"

I felt her hand glide across my shoulders as she circled me, then her nails trailed up my neck and under my jaw before vanishing from my skin. Half of me wanted her to hurry up and finish the song while the other half of me wanted her to tease me until I died from anticipation.

"Happy birthday, dear Lynne…"

I was desperate to taste her, but I knew she was just beginning and my wait was far from over.

"Happy birthday…to…you."

This was my Caroline, my sweet, the love of my life, and she had been planning this for weeks, dropping little hints to drive me crazy. It was my twentieth and she was determined to ring in this decade for me in a way I'd never forget. That was how I'd ended up in my current position, arms and legs tied to the chair; blindfold depriving me of my sight. I could still sense her though, and I knew she was aroused. When I breathed in, I could smell her faintly. I knew her eyes were watching me, and I felt more exposed than I'd ever been before, despite being fully clothed. She understood my body by now, knew the gentle slope of my petite breasts and the triangular patch of pubic hair I left above my snatch for ornamental reasons. She knew the easiest ways to make me come as well as how to hold me off until the last possible second.

There was a brief moment of silence once she finished the song, and I waited for something—*anything*—to happen. I thought I could feel her eyes burning holes through my clothes when I suddenly heard her footsteps leaving the room. The door closed slowly, and I sat there in amazement.

What was going on?

"Caroline?" I called out. I was confused but also very wet from the possibilities.

"Patience, lover!" she called back, and my confusion dissolved into excitement. What in the world had this girl planned? Here I was, sitting blindly in the middle of her bedroom, still wearing my work clothes (black skirt, white blouse, and no shoes) with my short red hair in wild disarrangement. My bare feet were getting cold on the hardwood floor, and I almost wished I could at least rub them together for warmth. Yet I was enjoying my bound, spread-eagle position.

The door creaked slightly as it opened again and her footsteps sounded somewhat different. Louder and sharper. Was she wearing heels? I was shocked. Caroline is wild and naughty, but has never shown her attitude in her clothing. Sometimes she wears these comfy knit shirts that cling to her chest beautifully and reveal the shadow of an areola, but that's the extent of her experimentation with erotic outfits. A smart, comfortable dresser, she tends to steer clear of anything too extravagant. So the sudden realization that yes, she was wearing heels (stilettos by the sound of it!), topped with the question of "What else is she wearing?" sent a delicious shiver throughout my body.

"I had to go get the rest of your gift," she explained as she reached me, her voice letting me know that she was standing a bit closer to me than I'd guessed.

I smiled in her direction...or where I *thought* she was. She moved slightly and I realized I could feel her breath on my face.

"Now you have three options, followed by one mandatory choice. Being the good person that I am—" I didn't even have to see her smirk to know it was there "—you will experience all three of your options in the end, but you get to choose the order."

It took all of my willpower not to move slightly and kiss her.

"You will only know your options as one, two, and three. They are in no particular order, but are all equally exciting. You do, however, get to know what that last mandatory option is in advance." She moved in even closer and I could smell the soft scent of her skin. Her voice lowered to a whisper. "No matter what order you choose, you will definitely get fucked tonight."

With that said, she ran the tip of her tongue over my upper lip, pulling away before I could return the favor.

Three choices with one invariable result; I could not go wrong.

"So what'll it be first?"

She was standing up again, waiting for my decision.

I licked my lips as I considered my options. They tasted like her.

"I suppose I'll go with number two first."

She chuckled softly.

"Good choice."

She stepped away from me, her heels click-clacking across the floor. Again, that feeling of vulnerability washed over me, and I realized I hadn't known I could feel this naked without actually being actually stripped bare. My loss of sight contributed to the sensation, as did my bound position, but I think a part of me *wanted* to feel so exposed. She had barely touched me, and I was already so turned on that I felt I could come at any moment.

I heard her rummaging with something on her...desk, yes that was in the direction she'd walked. There was silence, then the click-clack of her shoes as she made her way back to me.

For a second I thought my cell phone had gone off before I realized the buzzing was coming from whatever she had in her hands.

"As you've probably guessed, darling, behind door number two is a lovely new vibrator. Actually, a set of five."

Five? She'd gotten me five vibrators?

"Oh the wonders of Japanese technology." The buzzing sounded closer now. "They've invented these great finger attachments that will let me use my hands, with just a bit more of a punch than normal."

Her hand was so close to my neck that I could feel the air move slightly from the little minivibes. She lowered the toy gently onto my skin for a split second just to give me an idea of the sensation.

"But to really experience this correctly, one must use them on bare skin." She told me this matter-of-factly while the hand without the vibrators slowly undid the buttons on my shirt. She left a few buttons at the bottom done up, moving quickly to expose only my breasts. I could feel my nipples pressing against the material of my black bra, hard and ready for her touch. Caroline tilted my head back and the blindfold moved slightly, but offered me no more of a view than before. There was just the darkness, that hum, and her touch.

The second time she touched me with the vibrators, I could feel the individual pulsations coming from each finger. She started at my neck, slowly moving down to my chest, sliding over the top of my left breast, and circling around my still-covered nipple. The feel of the material of my bra coupled with the vibrations made my nipples ache with passion. She alternated breasts, still only touching very lightly. By the time she'd freed my breasts from the cups with her other hand, I was panting with excitement.

"Well, it looks like *you're* having fun...."

I nodded my head before the vibrations reached my bare nipple. The shock threw my head back and made my hands grip the chair tightly. This was unlike anything I'd ever felt before, and I knew I was close to coming but I needed her hands elsewhere.

Without warning, she removed both her hands from me. I moaned; I was so close! My head hung limply on my chest and I desperately tried to at least press my thighs together for some sort of friction. No luck, my legs were tied firmly apart.

I heard her walk over to the desk again. On her way back, she spoke. My head wavered blindly in the direction of her voice.

"Time to choose again."

I choose to be put out of this torment, I thought, *to be in her arms and to make her want me as much as I want her right now.* But that wasn't an option yet.

"One."

As she finally removed the blindfold, I blinked rapidly, realizing that there wasn't much light in the room to begin with. She had lit a bunch of candles and...what was she wearing?

My beautiful Caroline, most comfortable in khakis, was dressed in a black skintight PVC minidress, thigh-high fishnet stockings, towering stilettos, and black latex gloves that went past her elbows. Her blonde curls were loose and wild. She must have just put the gloves on because I would have noticed them against my skin. Her green eyes glittered mischievously as she waited for me to take in her total transformation. The dress flattered her ample breasts and juicy ass, cutting off midthigh before showing any cheek, though with a little movement it would probably reveal a lot more.

She turned and walked over to the stereo. I watched, mesmerized. Every step was a redefinition of the sexiest thing I'd ever seen. She reached out with that shiny, gloved hand to press the PLAY button. A soft song came on, low and sultry, and I faintly recognized the melody. It was some band from Montreal.

Walking back toward me, she gave me a wink and spoke. "Option number one is a striptease."

She closed her eyes for a second before beginning. Her body moved slowly, languidly, and just as I'd fantasized, the dress crept up as she danced. She came right up to me, her hands gliding across her chest, down her hips, and then back up to her inner thighs. I got a quick glimpse of bright red panties and moaned at the mere sight of them. I was beyond aroused and yet knew I still had one more door to open, one more choice to make.

She repeated these motions, in varying order, before her hands finally moved to the zipper at the top of the dress and pulled it down inch by inch by inch, so her bare chest was viewable to me. I could tell this was as much a turn-on for her as it was for me. Her eyes were closed and her body moved slowly and sensuously. She was the most amazing creature I'd ever seen.

Straddling me on the chair, she ground her body into mine. Her dress had already ridden up past her ass, and the motion of her movements pulled my own skirt up to expose my well-soaked panties. She smelled delectable, and I leaned forward to kiss her. But she pulled away and while still gyrating on me, leaned back until her head almost touched the ground behind her. Her body formed a perfect arch and her breasts slid past the material of her dress. Her nipples hardened as the cool air touched them, and I longed to envelop them with my mouth.

No such luck.

She sat up swiftly and lifted her weight off me as she stood. After undoing the rest of her zipper and letting the dress fall to the floor, my beautiful Caroline was exposed at last. Her skin shone golden brown, like a pot of honey and just as sweet. With curves from Victorian times, my large-bosomed beauty gracefully twirled and dipped for me. Slipping behind me swiftly, her hands snaked around my waist, then down my thighs to my knees, then back up again. The feel of the latex gloves against my skin was exquisite, as was the contrast between my pale thighs and their inky blackness. As she stroked my skin she whispered to me, "Looks like we've just got number three to do now."

I nodded, hoping it involved the release of this ache between my thighs.

She moved in front of me again and we both surveyed each other. She was still wearing those darling red panties, the stockings, shoes, and gloves. I knew I looked a mess, skirt hitched up almost to my waist, blouse half-open and my breasts pushed out above my bra. By the look in her eyes I knew she had me just the way she wanted me.

Wandering over to her desk yet again, she returned with something new in her hands: a beautiful blue dildo.

"This—" she waved it a bit "—is not for you...yet." Her smile was pure sex and wickedness. "This is for me...and for you to watch."

She backed toward the bed, then sat down and began to caress her breasts, stomach, and thighs. Finally, she slid her free hand down her panties. As she touched herself, I honestly believed I would tear the chair to bits before the night was over. My hands only clenched the armrest tighter as she kept going. I watched, transfixed, as she removed her hand from her panties just long enough to take them off. Then she lay back on the bed, completely exposing herself to me. Her beautiful shaved pussy was on display for my viewing pleasure.

By now, I knew how to make her come, but I had never watched her take care of herself. She didn't even bother to remove the gloves, and I wondered what they felt like on her skin, on her wet pussy lips.

She brought the dildo close to her pussy, then spread her lips and played the blue dildo over her slit. She slipped just a bit in, then pulled it out and rubbed the tip all over her clit. I could see how wet she was getting and this only made me wetter too. She pushed the dildo all the way in with one quick thrust, and her moan was the most glorious music I'd ever heard. I ground my pussy into the chair, looking for any kind of friction at all.

She thrust the dildo into herself hard and fast while playing with her clit. I knew she was getting close: her pussy was tightening and her breathing grew heavier and heavier.

"Lynne?" Her voice trembled when she called out my name. "I wish this was you...."

I groaned at her words and watched as she finally let go. Her cries were loud and delirious, her hips raised off the bed. I could almost feel her pussy contracting, could almost taste the juices flowing from her.

I waited for her to regain her senses as patiently as I could, considering the condition I was in. Slowly, ever so slowly, she sat up a bit and pulled the dildo out, her hands still trembling from the staggering orgasm.

It was only because of the surprised look she gave me that I realized I was whimpering from my need. "Caroline, I want to come."

Grinding my hips futilely against my seat just wasn't going to work. She moved quickly over to me, starting to take off the gloves.

"No!" I was almost frantic. "Leave them on."

She smiled as she knelt before me and started to undo the knots. Her lips finally found my own and she tasted like wine and candy and fruits I couldn't name. Her hands worked quickly and in a matter of seconds she had untied me.

She didn't pull away from my mouth as she slowly raised me out of the chair and onto the bed. My limbs slowly stretched out and relaxed, happy to be free from that chair. The relief was short lived, as my lust became even stronger than before. I began to move my hand down to finish myself off but she stopped me, the feel of the glove against my skin completely new. She put my hands at my sides and then worked at removing the rest of my clothing until I was finally as naked as I'd felt the whole time.

Once again, she trailed her fingers over my skin, letting me feel the tantalizing sensation of smooth latex. She caressed my body and built my passion up to its boiling point again. By the time she reached my clit, just a few quick rubs sent me over the edge. I came, screaming her name in one of the best orgasms of my life.

As I lay there, slowly coming down to earth, I reached over and took hold of the hand she'd used on herself. I slowly licked every drop of her off the slick material, enjoying her flavor immensely.

"Lynne—"

My eyes were still closed. When I opened them, I found her

staring at me adoringly. Uh-oh. She wasn't done with me yet. She still had something up her sleeve—or latex gloves, as it were.

Caroline moved her hand back between my thighs and slipped a single finger inside me. There was more than enough natural lube to work with so another finger easily went in. She pulled out very slowly before thrusting back in fast and hard. Just how I liked it. With every thrust, she pressed against my G-spot and her thumb brushed my clit roughly. With that combination, I wasn't able to hold out for long.

She muffled my cries with her mouth as I came the second time, my hips bucking wildly. She didn't even let me recover. Her hand kept up the pace and I had my third orgasm not even a minute later, collapsing, completely exhausted from the whole experience.

She took off the gloves, then her heels, before lying down beside me and covering us both with the duvet. I was still light-headed from it all.

I looked into her grass green eyes, completely in love and in lust with this woman. She just smiled and asked, "Well, how was that for a birthday present?"

I laughed and pulled her body closer to mine.

"I think that was a birthday to remember."

AMID FLOWERS

Debra Hyde

Cheryl picked up the phone and called William the day Barbaro fractured his ankle running the Preakness. It was something of a breaking point for Cheryl, representing one thwarted dream too many, and it had left her all too dismayed. The last Triple Crown winner had been Affirmed, a horse that had dueled repeatedly neck and neck against his rival, Alydar. That had been in 1978, the year Cheryl graduated college. When she picked Barbaro in the Derby and he won, hope soared. It would, after all, make a perfect fiftieth birthday present.

But Barbaro was in a cast, broken like her other dreams for Year Fifty. Like going to Paris and maybe snagging a bed at the famed Shakespeare and Company bookstore. Or visiting that Jamaican hedonists' getaway where she could spend her days naked and her nights lurid. Or even enjoying a quiet week, renting a beach cottage somewhere along the New England coast.

Unfortunately, repeated trips to Florida, first to see to her father's declining health, then to ease him into an assisted living facility, killed those possibilities. Having done right by her dad, Cheryl had absolutely no regrets, but it had exhausted the cash that could have taken her to Paris. In fact, it had taken enough time and cash to prevent any vacation to anywhere.

William, however, could soothe all this away. Maybe not permanently, maybe not ever for very long, but he knew how to unburden her. He knew how to be her balm.

"I'm glad you called," he said upon hearing her voice.

"That's an understatement," she told him. "You're so delighted, I can hear you grinning."

He laughed. "Well, what do you expect? I live for you."

Indeed, he did. William loved and adored Cheryl, so much that he overlooked the moody approach of her birthday, knowing, as an older man who had long ago seen his own fiftieth birthday, that what might first appear to be a mixed blessing of a milestone would, in short order, become rendered little more than a notable moment in her life. He knew that actual experience would mitigate anticipation.

That did not, however, mean that he would not do his part to make Cheryl's birthday pleasant and, hopefully, memorable. He had made arrangements that, if she were amenable, would allow him to pamper her and pleasure her.

"Listen," he prompted, "I know your plans didn't pan out as you wanted and I know that's been a disappointment. I can't promise you Paris or Jamaica, but I do have something in mind, if you're willing to let me whirl you away for the weekend."

Dear William, Cheryl thought. He would never think to keep her from her hopes and he never assumed that he would be invited into her plans, but he was ever willing to cater to her when it was most needed. Most men, when they claimed to be submissive, really needed a fantasy fix. They were driven by impulse and yearning and, while Cheryl never saw anything wrong with that, she truly appreciated William's ability to hang back and follow her lead—even if her lead did not include him. He always waited for her to call him to her side, however she needed him. And he never disappointed her.

That he offered a pampering was icing on the cake.

Icing on the cake, she thought. *Well, why not?*

"Sure. Yes," she agreed. "You always seem to know what I need."

William said nothing in return, but she could still hear him grinning.

The getaway was anything but a whirlwind. In fact, it was sedate and quiet and slow moving, consisting of a bed-and-breakfast stay in southern Connecticut, evenings at the casinos, and, according to William, other idylls that he would not divulge ahead of time.

"You'll have to wait for them to unfold," he informed her. "Some things have to be a surprise."

His first surprise came during a stroll on the grounds of the bed-and-breakfast. Calling the place a house was an understatement. Rather, it was a modest manor, big enough to have a fireplace and bathroom in every room; formal, structured gardens; an orchard; and wildflower meadows. To William, they were perfect for catering to Cheryl's needs.

He walked with a blanket rolled up under his arm, holding Cheryl's hand, and bearing a big dumb-luck smile on his face. Cheryl relaxed alongside the Zen of him, glad she had accepted his offer and glad that he had provided such a pleasant respite for her. When they came to a stone bench in the formal gardens, an old weathered thing shielded by a row of tall hedges, he spread the blanket over it and seated Cheryl there. He knelt before her and took her foot in his hand. Sliding her shoe off,

William began to massage her foot, firmly but with gentle concern for her comfort. He knew she was prone to toe cramps, as painful to her as the charley horses in his calves. Too hard a massage could provoke one.

Cheryl closed her eyes and enjoyed William's touch. She suspected he had all manner of scenarios planned for her, all of which would employ touch, some of which would provide release and relief. William knew what she needed and no matter how often she tried to make a strike for independence, she always came back to him. She could not go long without his touch; life always seemed to short-circuit when she tried to.

William worked the arch of her foot and smiled upward at her. He looked so beatific that Cheryl couldn't help but tease, "Is this more for you than me?"

"Maybe just a little bit," he admitted. "Although if it was really up to me, I'd have you push me away with your foot and scorn me, push me to the ground and trample me. But..." He kissed her foot. "I know better than that. I know not to be impetuous in the presence of a goddess."

"Oh hell," she countered. "You're just afraid of provoking a goddess's wrath."

"Sure I am. If I provoke you, you won't scorn and trample me. You'd do something far, far worse: you'd leave in disgust."

Truth be told, she could far more easily do the former than the latter. William was far too endearing and it was far too difficult to imagine him ever doing anything so disgusting as to provoke her departure.

William returned her shoe to her foot and helped her rise.

"Come," he beckoned, "I have something more to show you."

He led her from the formal garden and into the wildflower pasture that lay beyond it. At first, she hesitated to enter its tall grass—"Deer ticks," she told William, "and this sundress isn't exactly protection." But when William promised to check her thoroughly later, she did not resist this new adventure of his.

Cheryl estimated the field at ten acres and marveled at how beautifully the wildflowers grew there. For every daisy and aster she saw, she could also see the impending blooms of lupine and coneflowers. Birds swooped and sailed over the field and, when a blue streak flew past and landed on a field birdhouse, she pointed.

"A bluebird!"

William nodded and unrolled the blanket on the ground.

Cheryl reacted with horror. "Don't trample the flowers!"

But William assured her the flowers would pop back up, posing the question, "When was the last time you lay in an open field and let the world slowly go by?"

Cheryl didn't know—quite possibly she had never rested in an open field— and she let William ease her to the ground, deer ticks be damned.

Fair-weather clouds skimmed by on the light breeze, all so uniform in shape that one could not imagine a likeness in them, but Cheryl found their sameness calming. They went well with the fragrance of the field that wafted on the breeze, with the rustle of grass and flower alike. Peaceful, it was all so peaceful. *William*, she thought, *could not have thought of a better balm.*

Except he had. His hands crept up her thighs, his touch soft but electric and arousing, upward seeking as he gathered the skirt of her sundress and pushed it away. Cheryl tensed, but William cooed, assuring her that they were alone and unlikely to be discovered. Kisses followed his words and their goal became obvious as they inched upward.

Cheryl quivered as William's kisses mounted on her flesh and yearned for more. She grabbed him by his short locks, fingers digging into his scalp hard enough to make him gasp, a gasp that made her think of his cock, a tower of erect beauty and a source of great pleasure for her. But William's mouth angled to pleasure her first and when he reached her delta and placed his first kiss there, Cheryl trembled again.

Then, that exquisite touch of his tongue.

Briefly it licked her slit, just enough to make passage to its real goal, and when it landed upon her clit, Cheryl's cunt throbbed in acknowledgment. She arched her back, eager for his ministrations and, prompted, William spread her legs and plied his tongue.

Her taste was a rare delicacy, one worth savoring, and William worshipped her essence, careful to balance pleasuring her against his desire to linger between her legs for as long as possible. He flicked his tongue over her clit and swirled downward along her slit. He nipped lightly at her tempting, lavish lips, then worked his tongue into her. Cushioned splendor surrounded him, wet and flavored. Earthy, tangy, and delicious, it tempted William yet again to linger, but when Cheryl pulled him against her and set to grinding her hips against his face, he knew he had to heed her actions. William set his tongue to fucking, his mouth to lapping, a finger to rounding Cheryl's clit, and as he felt her arousal mount, his desire evaporated in the face of her lust. Now, he only wanted to please her.

And pleasing her meant making her come.

He worked with furious dedication. Every inch of tongue and every twist of his finger was his to give and, in giving it, he lost himself in these swirls of motion. He lost himself in Cheryl. Her mounting need rode him—his tongue, his fingers, his mouth—hard and hasty. She stampeded over him, a charger wild with lust and intent on breaking loose, running until she had what she sought: freedom in the pounding release of orgasm. She cried out as it took her, as throbs of ecstasy beat within, each one both ache and relief, itch and scratch converging in satisfaction. And in the wake of her ride, bliss came, softly, quietly, like the whisper of the breeze upon tall grass, a sigh that calmed her beast within, a welcome that beckoned it to slow itself and graze.

But Cheryl's animal was not yet ready to rest. Without a word, she pushed William from her and rose to kneeling. Rising on his elbow, William eyed her, curious and wondering. His answer came in her hand against his chest, pushing him over and onto his back. And it came in the prompt, nimble unbuckling of his belt. Cheryl opened his pants, just enough to fish his dick from hiding. Straddling him, she drove home her now perfectly clear intentions.

She took him with the same urgency that she had displayed when splayed before him, fucking him fast and feverishly, using him as if lust was a frantic thing to be captured and seized before it could flee. Where she was once the beast, now she was the hunter. Her quarry hid between her legs and under her busy fingers and only fucking could flush it out into the open.

The riotous rhythm of this fucking was a noisy business. Grunts guttural and gruff sounded from the impact of one body against another. Sweet, wet slurps issued as cunt rose from cock. Soft moans and sighs responded to fingers at work under a skirt, at cunt taking cock, at nipples hard under the hands that gripped a dress's bodice. And, in the heat of this hunt, Cheryl drove everything but the vain and glorious indulgence of pleasuring herself from her awareness. She lusted in the feel of William's cock, its thickness stretching her, its depth plumbing her. She lusted in the tight tingle of her clit against her finger, of her finger's rough rubbing. And in this blistering act, all her disappointments, her trials and tribulations, melted away, leaving Cheryl with only the joy of fucking, the wild need to reach and attain, and the satisfaction of quenching one's self.

In this zeal, a sudden peak battered Cheryl. It clenched at her, hurled her forward, and shook her within. But this time the hunter, Cheryl forced its capture. She continued to fuck and masturbate through the duration of her orgasm. She wrung every throb, every contraction, every groan and gasp from her coming, determined to conquer it and excise it from her, and she did not stop until exhaustion overtook her in the wake of her release.

Sapped of strength and drained of determination, Cheryl slid from William and slumped to the blanket, rag-doll limp and lolling. Minutes would pass before she roused to William's presence.

She found him still on his back, his pants splayed open, his cock now a limp and retreating remnant of its previously sturdy and sure spire. He had folded his arms behind his head and looked aloft, reminding her of a farm boy hiding in the hay and truant from his work. He looked like it, too, thanks to the shit-eating grin he bore. A happier dullard, you couldn't find.

Cheryl leaned over him and teased, "Sex makes you look stupid, you know."

Improbably, William's grin broadened, contorting his face into a caricature of itself.

"Stupid is as stupid does," he replied.

Truer words Cheryl had never heard and, adoring him, she roared with laughter before killing his grin in a hard and hearty kiss. As her tongue tangled with his, Cheryl realized that although William couldn't make all her dreams come true, he did chase all her sorrows and disappointments away. And, she realized, her long-held reluctance.

Days later, after much pampering and pawing, casino fun

and frolics, and more energetic sex, their long weekend drew to a close. They parted after a long, lingering kiss, in a farewell that promised reunion, soon and often. They had reached a turning point, one that had perched itself on Cheryl's birthday but was now ready to step beyond it: Cheryl decided that she would no longer resist William's dedication and desire to please her. William had taken her disappointment of a birthday and transformed it into an occasion of pleasure and joy, lust and passion, satisfaction and thankfulness, a feat by no means insignificant.

For Cheryl, that was gift enough—and, with William, so much more.

HER BIRTHDAY SUIT

Kate Laurie

"Stop looking so scared, Mina. You know I would never do anything to hurt you." Marcy's impatient reassurance did nothing to calm my fears.

"Will you at least tell me why I'm tied to the bed?" I asked my best friend hopefully. I sighed when there was no response. I had met her and Grace at the posh hotel expecting nothing more than my typical birthday present. Every year they would rent a room at a luxurious hotel and we would stay up all night drinking good wine and critiquing porn films. This time, however, as soon as I had entered the room, the two girls had blindfolded me and ushered me onto the king-sized bed. Then they had proceeded to tie my wrists and ankles to the bedposts with what felt like satin.

"I wish I could stay and watch, but I promised Marcy I wouldn't," Grace whispered to me excitedly.

"Wait," I urged her quietly. I struggled to hide a grin when

I heard her stop and then move closer. I tried to look terrified. "Please let me know what's happening," I begged pitifully.

"I can't."

"Won't you just tell me what the two of you are planning?" I held my breath as I waited for her to come to a decision.

"All right. But try to look surprised or Marcy will know that I didn't keep my mouth shut." I nodded in eager agreement. "In about five minutes a man will be arriving whose only instructions are to sexually please you in every imaginable way." She sighed. "I'm so jealous. I hope you guys are as creatively wicked when *my* birthday comes around." Just then Marcy came back into the room, so Grace hurried away.

I lay on the bed in shock. I'm not a sexually inhibited person, and this was every girl's fantasy. But my lack of control frightened me. The idea of being bound to the bed and subject to the desires of a stranger made me tremble. "Can you please come over here, Grace?" I called in a voice that shook just a tiny bit.

"What is it, Mina?" Grace asked cheerfully.

"Closer," I whispered, lowering my voice until she had to sit on the bed beside me to hear it. "How do you know this guy isn't a psycho?"

"We would never leave you in the hands of a stranger!" Grace assured me in a shocked voice. "Don't worry. It's someone we trust to take care of you very carefully and thoroughly." After uttering those confusing words, she left again.

I frowned as I mentally replayed what she had said. Someone they knew and trusted. I almost would have preferred a stranger. I considered our male acquaintances. Not one seemed like the type of man they would have chosen to approach about something this bizarre and personal. A knock on the door scattered my thoughts and sent my heart racing.

"Come in and make yourself comfortable," Marcy's low

voice called out happily. She let out a throaty laugh. "Is that your bag of goodies?"

I assume he must have nodded.

"I'm glad to see that you've come well prepared."

What had he brought? I struggled against my bonds one more time to no avail. I heard heavy footsteps coming toward me, and then a large hand stroked my face. I froze and struggled to breathe normally.

"Don't struggle so, darling. These scarves are made of silk, but you'll still bruise your wrists if you struggle too much." He continued to brush my hair back from my face as he said this. His voice was deep and textured like red wine, and it was also vaguely familiar. I struggled to place it but came up blank. I jumped a little as he sat on the bed, and I felt the press of a jeans-clad leg against my side. I opened my mouth to speak, but he beat me to it.

"Good-bye, ladies. I should be gone by early tomorrow morning, but you may want to wait until noon or so before coming up. I have a feeling that Mina may be bit tired tomorrow." He ran his hand down my arm as he said that and I felt my skin prickle with goose bumps in its wake.

"Take good care of her tonight," Marcy instructed the mysterious man sternly. "Don't hold back at all, no matter how much she begs. I want this to be a one-night stand like no other for our Mina."

"Bye, honey, you can thank us tomorrow," Grace called out with a giggle as she shut the door behind them.

I wanted to cry out for them to come back, but I didn't. I knew that there wasn't a single thing I could say or do that would cause Marcy to change her mind. Instead, I turned to my captor with what I hoped was a winsome smile. "I won't say a word to them if you let me go. I'll make up an outrageously seductive story they'll believe, and I'll even pay you twice whatever they're paying," I offered hopefully. I felt his hands on my ankles and experienced a brief surge of triumph. It faded when he simply tugged off my sandal. He moved to my other foot and did the same thing.

"A promise is a promise. I can't leave until you are absolutely satisfied." He punctuated the statement with a small kiss to my ankle that sent chills racing up my body and caused a traitorous clenching between my thighs. He laughed as if aware of my reaction, then casually asked, "Is that a favorite outfit you're wearing?"

It took me a moment to register what he had said since it seemed so irrelevant. "No, actually it's not. It's just comfortable." I found myself trying to justify it, and I rolled my eyes in disgust. There was no reason for me to defend my choice of clothing to this man.

"Good," he answered shortly and then I felt a touch of cold metal on my skin and heard the sound of fabric tearing.

"What the hell are you doing?" I asked furiously. He didn't answer and didn't stop. I felt him cut through the waist and down the front of the long skirt I had worn. Then he lifted my rear up and swept the fabric out from under me and began cutting off my tank top. "Stop right this minute. Aren't you supposed to be seeing to my pleasure?"

"How am I going to do that when you're fully clothed?" he asked with a sexy laugh.

I decided not to respond, tensing when I felt the scissors slide against my hip as he cut the sides of my panties. I felt a shiver of apprehension and hoped my friends were right to trust this man. A moment later, he snipped the straps of my bra and undid the clasp. He slipped the garment off my shoulders and I cursed the vulnerability of my position. I wanted to murder Marcy and Grace.

"I really wish you wouldn't struggle so. The last thing I want is for you to chafe your wrists."

I forced myself to stay still, and I listened to the sound of him undressing.

"I want you to know that I'm not going to anything that you truly do not want tonight. This doesn't mean that you can just tell me to go home. It means that if there are particular pleasures that you are uncomfortable with just tell me and I will stop. Now, why don't I get to know your body a little better?" Indeed as soon as he finished his speech, he slid his nude body next to mine and rested his hand on my damp mound. "Oh good, I expected that this would excite you," he laughed in delight.

"Are you going to let me take off my blindfold?" I asked him calmly. I was struggling not to react to the long fingers that teased my plump lips. I was ashamed of my body's easy desire. Already I felt the tips of my breasts tightening and more moisture gathering below.

"No, Mina, that is something I can't allow. You know me, and I don't think you'd be able to experience the pleasure as freely if you knew who I was." He paused and ran his hand in a long caress from my shoulder to my hip. "It would be difficult for both of us after as well, and I don't want to cause you any awkwardness."

I was becoming more confused by the minute. So he was someone I still saw at least occasionally, and he didn't think I'd be able to enjoy myself as much if I knew who he was. I suddenly lost the ability to think reasonably as he leaned over and licked one of my tight nipples with his tongue. I cried out despite myself.

"Yes, Mina, that's the type of sound I want to hear from you tonight. No more questions and no more worries. Now, I'm going to give you a massage to relax you." He scooted down to the bottom of the bed and placed his hand on my ankle. "Can I trust you not to kick me?"

"I won't kick you," I promised quickly. I was feeling more aroused by the moment, and I no longer had any desire to escape.

He untied the scarf from around my ankle and placed my foot in his lap. I couldn't help but move my foot a little in a small upward stroke along his inner thigh. He laughed but said nothing. He leaned across me and I felt the rasp of his pubic hairs against the sole of my foot. Curious as to his endowment I attempted to investigate with my foot, but this time he caught my foot with his hand.

"No more of that now, Mina. I'm about to rub oil into your feet and calves, and it would be hard for me to concentrate if you kept that up. So please be good, and perhaps I'll be able to untie you completely." He slipped one oiled hand up my calf and leaned forward to plant a chaste kiss on my upper thigh. "Promise me you'll be good, Mina."

I shivered in anticipation and desire, but I managed to squeak out a quiet reassurance: "I'll be good." I couldn't prevent a moan of delight as I felt his large warm hands begin working on my foot. He was using a liberal amount of the oil, and it felt divine. When he ran his blunt fingernails across my arch I felt my entire body jerk in a combination of pleasure and surprise. He removed his hands and I attempted to sit up, forgetting the restraints for a moment. "Please don't stop," I told him breathlessly. "I promise not to move at all."

"I'm just pouring more oil into my hands so I can start on your calf." He slid both his hands all the way up my leg, stopping just before my wet and swollen lips. He gave a small laugh and his breath caused my clitoris to swell in impatient desire. "At least I can be reasonably assured that my services have been appreciated so far."

He poured a small puddle of oil onto my shin and I sighed at its delicious warmth. He lifted my foot into his lap again and began easing all the tight muscles in my calf. He had amazingly sexy hands. They were long fingered and strong with just a hint of calluses. The rough texture of his fingertips felt delicious against the silkiness of the oil and the sensitive smoothness of my skin. He poured some more oil onto my thigh and began rubbing it in the most leisurely way imaginable. It was driving me mad with lust. I had thought that his hands on my calves were heaven, but this was hell. Every sweep of his large hands brought him higher.

"I'm relaxed enough. I command you to bring me satisfaction now." I felt like a fool as I stated the request imperiously, but I attempted to maintain a look of haughty dignity beneath my blindfold. I gasped when he slid a slick hand up my thigh and teased the crease that separated my desire from its fulfillment.

"Sorry, I am here to pleasure you, that's true enough. I was instructed, however, to bring you to release only when it would be unbearably cruel to wait a moment longer, and I think a little more anticipation will do you good." He began massaging my thigh again, but then he paused and said, "But I could give you a little something to tide you over, since my desire probably matches your need."

Then he leaned forward and my world exploded.

His tongue was the most divine thing to ever touch me. He found my pulsing clit on the first try and I embarrassingly climaxed immediately. His tongue was incredibly flexible. I found myself wishing I could take back my orgasm in order to keep that exquisite torture continuing. He didn't stop, however, and as he expertly alternated between kissing my lips and my clit he brought me to the cusp once again. I thrashed as much as was possible within my binds, and cried out unintelligible encouragements. Then he stopped. I gasped for air and waited desperately for his damp mouth to return but was disappointed.

"You taste wonderful," he told me, slightly breathless. "I hope you're ready for a long night," he warned me with mock sternness. "I had promised myself to resist bringing you to climax for at least three hours, and it's only been one hour."

He pinched my clit between his fingers and I bucked my hips in an unpreventable response. "I couldn't resist you though. All spread out on the bed, with your pink lips all swollen and dripping wet beneath your damp curls. I tried to ignore you, but I've wanted you too long." He snapped his mouth shut after this, and I realized that he'd given away more than he meant to.

"Are you sure you won't let me take the blindfold off?" I begged him piteously. I was amazingly curious now. There was something absolutely exhilarating about knowing that a man had secretly lusted after my body and now he had been given the chance to act out all of his fantasies. I couldn't imagine anyone I knew being capable of the expert foreplay this man was exhibiting. I once again racked my brain for possibilities but this man seemed much too sensual and experienced to be anyone of my acquaintance.

"Sorry, darling, I can't do that." He dropped his voice down until I could feel it like liquid silk all over my body. "Don't you think it adds to the experience? A little helplessness and intrigue thrown in for spice? I have you completely at my mercy and you must rely on the judgment of your two friends and none of your own. I find your unconquerable passion quite exhilarating myself," he confessed into my ear. A chill ran down my body and I felt my nipples tighten to a point of near pain. "So how old are you now, Mina?"

I forced myself to focus enough to answer.

"I will be twenty-six at ten till midnight." I gasped when I felt his hands smooth the warmed oil all over my sensitive breasts. "Oh, god."

He laughed and rolled both of my aching nipples at once. "No more talking, Mina. The only sounds I will accept for the next few hours are those of passion. Now relax and enjoy your birthday present." I was about to explain that I would talk if I wanted to but just then he pressed my breasts together and took both of my nipples into his mouth at once. I decided he was right. This was a once-in-a-lifetime opportunity and I was going to take advantage of it.

For the first time I was actually glad for the blindfold. While he leaned over me and teased my nipples mercilessly I scooted as far down on the bed as my restraints would allow. I began to rub desperately on his thigh. I felt him take his mouth off my nipples in surprise.

"Move a little closer. I need more friction," I gasped out. He silently acquiesced, even shifting over a little until I had perfect access. I groaned in approval and quickly achieved a delicious rhythm against his muscular leg.

I was strung so tight I thought I'd explode. All of my skin seemed to be on fire tonight. Being deprived of my sight made all of my other senses work overtime, and it was driving me wild. I relished the taste of the sweat on my upper lip. The salty tang of my skin mixed with our mutual desire to produce an exotic musk that I breathed in gratefully. The greatest increase was to my sense of touch. It felt as though I had a million sensory nerves in every inch of my skin. The sensitivity that I normally only felt on my breasts, thighs, and neck had spread until my entire body quivered with every touch. He leaned over and licked my lower stomach and I bucked my hips in ecstasy. His long tongue traced delicate designs onto my skin that caused my toes to curl with delight.

He began kissing a slow line of heat down my stomach until he stopped just above my thatch of brown curls. I thrust upward in desperation.

"Guess what, Mina? It's almost midnight. Happy birthday," he whispered, the last words uttered right against my sex and the slight vibration of his mouth causing my hips to buck and my head to fall back in frustration.

"Please fuck me," I begged him. I wanted nothing more than to be filled to bursting by a large and thick cock. I just hoped he'd measure up to my needs.

"I'll do even better," he promised me mysteriously. He gave me one long slow lick that made me shiver. I frowned when I felt his weight leave the bed.

I heard him rummaging around in what I guessed was the bag that Marcy had referred to earlier tonight. Tonight? It was hard to believe that I had only been tied up for a few hours. It felt as though this had been my entire existence. This mix of pleasure and anxiety was intoxicating. I bit my lip as I wondered what he would do next.

"Lift your hips a little," he told me as I felt him sit down next to me again. I obeyed, and he slipped a firm pillow beneath my lower back. I was now displayed quite obscenely for him, and I jumped a bit when I felt him spreading lubricant over my anus. "Shh, if you don't like it I'll take it out."

"Take what out?" I gasped as my question was answered. He slowly slipped a small dildo into me. I experimented by rocking my hips forward and was surprised when I felt it flex inside of me.

"What is that?" I gasped out.

"It's filled with oil so that it will contract and flex in time to your thrusts. Do you like it?" he asked me curiously. I nodded in response and I could almost see his grin when he replied. "Great, we are ready to begin then."

I was about to ask what we were going to begin, but I didn't get a chance. He untied my other foot, kissed my ankle where the scarf had been tied and then hoisted both of my legs onto his shoulders. His skin was incredibly hot and as he slid up toward me I smiled to find that he was covered in a fine sheen of sweat. He thrust his middle finger into me, and I jerked up sharply causing the dildo to rock pleasurably inside me. He began to tease my clitoris with his tongue and I threw my head back in amazement. This was the most exquisite feeling imaginable. Once again I felt as though I might actually explode. I wasn't surprised when I climaxed almost immediately. He didn't even pause, however. He was working in a taxing rhythm that didn't give me a moment of relief. The dildo was a steady pressure from behind and his finger was just long enough to press into me at almost the same exact spot. The feeling of being filled from both directions would have been enough to bring me to a second shattering climax all on its own, but when he added his skilled tongue into the mix again it was nearly too much. It wasn't until my third climax had left me shivering and drenched in sweat that he stopped.

I was languorous and completely sated. I looked at him and gave a slow sleepy smile. I blinked as I recognized Marcy's cousin, Jude. I felt my mouth drop open as I realized that my blindfold must have slipped off during one of my shuddering orgasms. He had his eyes closed as he rested his head on my upper thigh. I admired his sexy mouth and tousled black hair for a moment before I spoke up, "Why Jude, you could have done this for my birthday long ago."

Jude sat straight up in surprise. He met my eyes and winced. "Are you mad at me, Mina?" he asked hesitantly.

I looked at him in silent appraisal. His upper body was gleaming with sweat and his mouth was wet from my own juices. I licked my lips and sighed. "Not at all. Now are you ready to come up here and fuck me for real?" I purred.

He looked up at me in amazement and then grinned. "With pleasure." He reached above me and untied both of my wrists. He entered me with one swift thrust that brought me to the edge once again. I smoothed my hands down his muscular back and then gripped his hips.

He pounded into me with abandon, causing the dildo to tease me relentlessly. I was amazed when I came for the fourth time that night, and more than a little grateful to my friends for setting the whole thing up. I flung my arms out to the sides and peered up at Jude with a look of contemplation. "I hope you know I'll be expecting this on more days than my birthday," I warned him.

"I think that can be worked out," he promised me gravely. "In fact," he told me as he entered me again, "I think I'll start right now."

VERONICA'S LOVER

Anonymous

Veronica's lover had tied her to the bed faceup with leather restraints around her wrists and ankles, leaving just enough give in the ropes lashed to the head- and footboard so that Veronica could struggle deliciously. Veronica's sight was blocked with a padded leather blindfold padlocked around her head, but she was not gagged.

"Anything," Veronica had told her lover. "Anything at all. You can do anything to me."

Which might have been a dangerous request for her birthday, if Veronica hadn't allowed her lover to read her diary. Veronica's diary was not like most other diaries; hers was a multivolume collection of erotic fantasies, ranging from the sublime to the extreme. She knew, because she knew her lover so well, that tonight, on her birthday, she would be forced—*forced* was the word that excited her when she was tied up like this, though she wanted nothing more than to *be* forced, making it a strange word to use—to experience one of those fantasies.

But which one? One of her fondest, a fantasy that she had written and rewritten in a dozen incarnations throughout the hundreds of pages tucked into loose-leaf binders? Or one of the scary ones, a fantasy she had written in a moment of audacious extremity and forgotten about entirely till now, one that would terrify and excite her as she groped in her memory for every detail she had written down?

Her breath came fast as she heard the bedroom door opening and closing.

She heard soft footsteps approaching the bed, took a deep breath and smelled an unfamiliar body—a stranger. Perfume, just a hint of it, mingled with the scent of sex, her own and the stranger's. She felt the weight on the bed and her body tensed as smooth fingers ran up her body, touching first her thighs, then her wet pussy, making her gasp and squirm as she felt herself penetrated, invaded; as she felt her clit teased. Then the hand, now moist with Veronica's own juices, trailed its way up Veronica's belly and over her breasts, squeezing them, pinching her nipples—then, quite unexpectedly, traveling to Veronica's face so the fingers, slick with pussy, could be forced between Veronica's parted lips.

She licked, savoring her own juices. She felt a hot mouth on one nipple, suckling it, making it stiffen more as her pussy responded with pulses that matched the strokes of the stranger's tongue.

When the hand and mouth left her, Veronica longed for them back. A mouth pressed to hers, tasting different than her lover's, different than any mouth she'd ever tasted. She felt a tongue, long and lithe, pressing its way into her mouth, opening her up, preparing her. Then Veronica felt the weight shifting atop her, the stranger changing position, her knees tucked alongside Veronica's upper torso, calves underneath Veronica's upper arms. Smooth thighs surrounded Veronica's face, caressing her cheeks as the stranger's crotch made its way down onto Veronica's face.

She smelled it, sharp and tangy.

Sex. Female sex. She felt it wriggling, descending as the thighs pressed tighter against her, forcing this stranger's pussy against Veronica's open mouth, stifling her panting moans with the inexorable press of moist folds of flesh.

Veronica felt a surge of arousal go through her nude body as her tongue found the strange woman's entrance. The taste was so unfamiliar to her, so new and exotic. Hungrily, she began to feed, her tongue licking from the woman's smooth, slick opening to her clit, listening to the faint moans of ecstasy as she began to work the woman's firm bud. Apparently she had mounted the bed with her ass toward Veronica, because as Veronica lapped at the woman's pussy she felt an unfamiliar mouth on her own cunt, so helpless and vulnerable between her open thighs. Veronica's moans were muffled by the strange woman's pussy as she felt a tongue working its way between her lips. She felt the tip of that tongue pressing her clit.

Veronica felt the electric charge exploding through her, her arousal mounting as her ass lifted off the bed. The woman was larger than her, and her weight bore Veronica back down into the bed. Veronica ate her pussy hungrily as the woman ground her hips rhythmically in time with Veronica's ministrations. Meanwhile, the woman found the perfect rhythm on Veronica's cunt, and Veronica sank desperately into pleasure, giving herself over to it.

Was Veronica's lover watching her? Standing in the doorway savoring Veronica's surrender? Had her lover trained a video camera on her, to capture this moment for later enjoyment?

Or was this moment Veronica's alone—Veronica's, and the stranger's?

Slender fingers worked their way into Veronica's pussy; she gasped as their soft pads hit her G-spot firmly and began to massage it. Veronica squirmed against the bonds, each movement of her body accenting both the suckling hunger of her mouth and the press of the strange woman's tongue on her clit—not to mention the rush of unexpected pleasure deep in her pussy. Veronica was going to come. She knew it. But she wanted this woman to come, too; she wanted to pleasure the stranger as much as the stranger was pleasuring her.

To her surprise, as Veronica licked harder, suckling on the woman's clit, the fingers left her and the pussy-slick hands gripped her thighs, as the strange woman's hips began to buck and pump. Veronica licked faster, not letting up until the woman had shuddered and climaxed on top of her, moaning uncontrollably with each stroke of Veronica's tongue.

Then, with a gasp, she lifted her pussy off of Veronica's face, unable to bear any more stimulation. Veronica's mouth still worked involuntarily, her tongue lolling out to lick after the pussy denied her. Then her mouth went slack as she felt the fingers pushing into her again, as she felt the mouth descending on her pussy again. As she felt the tongue on her clit and her entire body exploded in sensation.

It took moments, this time; the feel and sound and smell and taste of the woman climaxing on top of her had driven Veronica over the edge. In the moments before her orgasm, she wondered again if her lover was watching, if her lover had arranged to savor this moment later—or if this orgasm, this intense climax that was about to explode through her, was hers alone—hers and the stranger's.

Veronica felt her muscles spasming, the first hint that she was coming. Then, a split second later, the pleasure burst through her naked, bound body and she let out an unrestrained wail of ecstasy, her whole body shaking as she released herself into the stranger's touch. She felt the room spinning, unseen, as she lost herself in the sensations and bright lights exploded in her eyes behind the blindfold.

Still whimpering, Veronica felt the strange woman licking her pussy clean, devouring the juices that had leaked onto her thighs. When she felt the woman rising, Veronica took a great sobbing breath and felt the cold of the room hit her, the woman's body heat having vanished in an instant. She wanted to lift her head and look—to see if her lover was there—but she could see only blackness, the smooth inky blackness of the leather blindfold.

Veronica heard footsteps. Two sets of them. One, getting further away.

One set of footsteps, coming closer.

She heard the door being opened, a silent pause, and then the sound of it closing.

She took a deep breath, smelled the familiar scent. She felt her lips parting in a rapturous smile, heard herself whispering her lover's name.

Heard the greeting returned, "Veronica" whispered, soft and close. Tasted the familiar kiss on her lips.

Veronica felt the weight as her lover mounted the bed, heard the bed creak as she strained upward against the bonds, wanting to savor the weight atop her. That weight bore her into the bed, and Veronica surrendered to it.

TWENTY-NINE AGAIN

Emilie Paris

She was turning twenty-nine.

Again.

Twenty-nine, for the fourth straight year. And it was becoming increasingly difficult to get away with what had started out as a little white lie. Difficult to create a new circle of friends each year who would buy her age, who would celebrate with her, celebrate wildly, as if the world would end at thirty. Somehow, she'd known this would happen, had predicted it back when she'd blown out twenty-nine candles for the first time. Known in her soul that twenty-nine was the number to be, the number to stay.

Slowly, she looked around the apartment. Todd's apartment. He'd offered to throw the bash for her here, and most of the friends in attendance were his. She liked his place, near the beach, with the balcony overlooking the white sands. White sands at night, anyway, beneath the glowing light of the full moon. Venice Beach was perfect for a little bohemian get-to-gether. The guys in their long Hawaiian-print board shorts and Sex Wax shirts were all about Todd's age, midthirties; the girls were far younger than Angie. Little surfer girls, who thought twenty-five was ancient, and twenty-nine the absolute end of the road. You're thirty? Out to pasture you go. They snuck pitying peeks at her as they tied up their silky halters and adjusted their tiny little minis to reveal acres of tanned skin.

Angie looked as good as they did. She knew it. But looking good took more effort now. Her blonde hair was foiled every six weeks to get the sun-kissed gold streaks that framed her pretty, heart-shaped face, which emphasized the metal in her bronze-brown eyes. Her tan was equally manufactured, carefully applied all over her body, after a rigorous loofah bath. She never went in the sun anymore if she could help it. Didn't dare. Still, in the mirrored mantel over the unused fireplace, she saw a kid when she caught her reflection.

Twenty-four, maybe. Nineteen even, if one were to squint.

"You look amazing," one of the girls smiled at her as she refilled Angie's glass of bubbly, seeming to read Angie's mind.

"You do," Todd agreed aloud, before bending to add in a whisper, "Not a day over thirty-three."

"What do you—" Angie stammered, her heart pounding, but he just shook his head and lifted the clear green bottle of Rolling Rock to his lips to hide his grin. Generally, she loved his smile, loved the way it made her feel inside, but this was different. Impish, somehow. Sly. Without another word, he headed over to the knot of friends gathered around the chips and dip. Was he messing with her? Did he know for real?

She'd worked so hard. *Too* hard. Last year, she'd spent her birthday with a man from her gym, a trainer, and several of his buddies, out on a boat in Marina del Rey. No one had thought to challenge her for real. To grill her on what music she'd listened to in high school, what year she'd been born. But just in case, she had all of the math memorized. Last year, she'd been born in 1976. The Bicentennial. That was easy enough to remember.

Each year, for the month prior to her birthday, she quizzed herself as she got ready for work, staring at her reflection in the mirror as she brushed her teeth and did her makeup, going over the pertinent facts for the hour it took her to primp.

To be twenty-nine this year, she'd been born in 1977. She'd graduated high school in '95 and college in '99. Didn't seem like too much to learn, but things like that made a big difference in conversation. Small talk often veered to dates, which she'd learned the hard way, having to play dumb on her second twenty-ninth birthday when she'd messed up and gotten the year of her high school graduation wrong, having to cover up by saying she'd gone abroad for a year and had to retake the seventh grade.

Todd brushed her shoulder with one big hand, and she looked up at him, catching the glimmer in his eye, wondering if he knew for real, or if he was only fucking with her.

"Let's go out on the balcony," he suggested, and she followed him, feeling meek, cowed, even as one of the giggling girls set a little sparkling silver tiara in her glossy hair. A princess. For one night a year, that's all she wanted. You couldn't be a princess in your thirties, could you?

"It's beautiful," she sighed as she watched the waves lap the shore.

He nodded, wrapping her in his strong embrace, which made her feel safe, normally, but now put her off balance as she couldn't see his amber eyes.

"Why'd you lie?"

Again, her heart throbbed. He knew.

"I—"

"Nothing wrong with being in your thirties."

"There is in L.A."

"But you're not a starlet. There's no expiration date on being a curator."

Yes, he was right. She could organize exhibitions at the gallery until she was one hundred, and she knew it. But somehow thirty had seemed like the year that she was supposed to have all of her shit together. Thirty meant she was supposed to stop buying four-hundred-dollar shoes, stop living frivolously, stop spending on her clothes what she should be putting into a 401K plan, and she could bear none of that.

"I'm thirty-eight," he reminded her.

She nodded. She knew it. He'd told her his age when he bought the painting right out of the gallery window, the one that was now hanging on the wall in his entryway. Todd had said in their first conversation that he'd finally made it to a point where he had a little extra for the things he'd always dreamed of. He'd bought the picture as a birthday present for himself, and he hadn't paused or coughed or hid the fact that he was nearing forty.

"Men are different," she told him, matter-of-factly. It was true. He must understand that. A man could be sixty and date a girl in her twenties and nobody blinked an eye. Look at Jack Nicholson and Lara Flynn Boyle or Harrison Ford and Calista Flockhart. But you never saw it the other way around. There were different rules for men than there were for women. Even Todd, who worked with numbers all day long, keeping track of finances on movie sets, wasn't going to try to argue that fact with her, was he?

"But what were your plans? Next year, you wouldn't have

been able to tell me you were twenty-nine again."

She remained silent. That was the biggest problem. She couldn't have stayed with him. She had to move on. New circle of friends. New circle of lies. The way she was no longer with the trainer from last year, or the hack screenwriter from the year before, or the film editor with whom she'd spent years twenty-seven, twenty-eight, and the *real* twenty-nine.

He turned her to face him. "You were going to dump me?"

She saw the hurt in his eyes and quickly shook her head. They hadn't been going out long enough for her to think that far ahead. Two and a half months. Not a real relationship yet. She didn't even have any of her clothes at his place. Yet he seemed to be waiting for a response.

"I don't know," she said. "I would have played it by ear."

"And if we'd lasted, you would have turned thirty next year, then thirty-one, and forever after you'd have had to try to remember the fake you—"

She shrugged. She'd just never thought that far ahead. "How'd you find out anyway?"

"I knew from the start. Saw your driver's license when we were getting into that club in Hollywood. I work with numbers, you know. I did the math. Addition comes automatically for me."

And she remembered. She'd been carded, which was thrilling, and she hadn't considered Todd a keeper at the time, so she hadn't worked hard enough to hide it from him. How had it slipped her mind? She was usually so careful.

"And then, when you said you were turning twenty-nine, my interest was piqued, so I kept quiet."

And he'd let her run with it, making a complete and total fool of herself—

"Is that the only lie you've told me?"

She looked into his eyes again, dark brown eyes, and she thought she saw a deepness there, an understanding, that she hadn't seen before. He was asking her this for a reason. Not to mess with her, but because he really wanted to know. And he wanted to know because he—oh, she didn't want to think it, because that might jinx it.

"I want to know," he said, flat out, "because I need to trust you."

"Yes," she stammered, "that's the only time."

"Good," he nodded. "Because I can see a real future for us, Angie. But not if you lie."

A real future. That went with the real life. That went with the fact that she'd been born in 1973 not '77, that she could actually remember the fireworks from the Bicentennial, proof positive that it wasn't the year of her birth.

He looked at her soberly, and she wondered what he was thinking. There was no way to read his eyes. "But if we're going to be honest," he said, "I need to tell you something, too."

She waited, wondering. "You're sixty," she finally grinned.

"No," he shook his head. "I didn't go into that gallery just to buy the picture," he said. "I'd seen you in there for a month before I got up the nerve to come inside. I would have walked out with you instead of the picture if I could have."

The best birthday present, she started to think, was to be with him. The rest of it, all of it, the numbers and the dates, were things that she could spin around in her head so that she wouldn't have to pay attention to what was really going on close by her. That wasn't to say she was unfocused. At work, she could create the most coherent shows, arranging the pictures just so, spending hours sweating over the smallest details. Art was easy. Real life was difficult.

She watched the partiers through the sliding glass door, and she didn't feel any longing to join them. Running around playing younger than she actually was suddenly seemed far less important. Being with Todd was what mattered.

"But we do have to deal with the fact that you lied—" Todd said, bringing it all around again.

For the third time that evening, her heart pounded so hard that she felt he might be able to hear it.

"With a birthday spanking—"

Oh, god—

"One for each and every year."

She lowered her head, but he caught her chin in one hand and lifted her face to his.

"You agree with the terms?"

So meek she was, even wearing a tiara, like a princess. "Yes," she finally managed to say. "Yes."

"When they leave," he nodded toward the window, indicating his slew of beautiful guests, "when the last one leaves, I mean, you'll bend over my lap and take it like the naughty birthday girl you are—"

She said nothing, eyes locked on his, feeling a burst of nervousness mingled with a wave of anticipation flood through her.

"You understand?" His voice was so deliciously strict she could have come right then with very little assistance.

"Yeah," she finally managed. "Yes, Todd."

It was hell waiting. She found herself mingling with the partiers, laughing, telling stories, but keeping an eye on the clock the whole time. They'd all have to leave by one, wouldn't they? Or two at the latest. She watched Todd surreptitiously. He wasn't drinking anymore. Didn't have a bottle of beer in his hand for the rest of the night. Was he as excited as she was? She couldn't tell from his poker face.

At one point in the evening, she sat on the edge of Todd's sofa and chatted with several of the young girls. She'd never really talked with them before, she'd only looked at them enviously, considered them the competition. It was a surprise to learn that they were interested in art, to find from their comments that they actually looked up to her. She'd never thought of things like that. That youngsters might actually want to have what she had. A top job in a stellar gallery. A closet full of Manolos and Louboutins.

"And your dress," one of the little girls cooed. "I love your dress."

"Wish I could afford one of those," her friend sighed. "Can't buy anything over the Gap or Contempo on my salary."

She remembered what that was like, a decade ago when she first was starting out. Remembered thrift-store shopping and borrowing clothes from her buddies. New thoughts flooded through her mind all night, but each one would eventually hit the wall of "birthday spanking"—and she'd look over at Todd. He always seemed to be looking back at her, sending a fresh wave of nerves through her, even when all he did was smile.

Finally, the last couple left, and she and Todd were alone. From the stern expression on his face, Angie thought he might give her a talking to, and then, when he didn't say a word, she thought he might let her off the hook. But Todd had his own plans. He simply gripped her wrist and pulled her over to the sofa, bent her over his lap, and lifted the patterned Diane von Furstenberg wrap dress all the way up to her hips.

She had on lilac lace-edged La Perla panties underneath the thin wrap—panties she'd chosen with thoughts of an entirely different postparty event—but Todd didn't pause to admire the expensive knickers. He let one hand come down firmly on her ass, and Angie jumped at the unexpected sting. It had never occurred to her that he was going to treat this as a real, punishment spanking, but clearly he was. Todd spanked her other cheek just as hard, and she yelped, doing the math suddenly in her head. Two. He'd only given her two. And she had—Christ, thirty-one to go.

"Liar," Todd hissed as his hand landed a particularly stinging blow to the undercurve of her ass. "This is what happens to bad little birthday liars."

"I'm sorry," she managed to whisper.

"No," he said, his voice rich with a dark humor. "You're not yet. But you will be." And he was right. He spanked her steadily on her panty-clad ass until she felt tears form in her eyes. Then, when she thought he was giving her a break, he surprised her even further by pulling her panties down her thighs and spanking her bare flesh.

How far was he going to take this, she wondered? Was he actually going to make her sob?

Todd had a hard hand, and he used it to advantage against the lush curves of her ass. She knew that she'd have a difficult time sitting down the next day, would be sleeping on her stomach that night, no sheets necessary to keep her warm. The heat of her ass would do the job just fine.

When he reached thirty-three, she felt relief cascade over her, but Todd didn't let her up. "Don't forget," he murmured.

"Forget?"

"One to grow on," he said, before landing the firmest blow of the evening, right on her sweet spot.

Angie cried out at the pain, and Todd immediately slipped her panties all the way off her lean legs, and then swung her around in his embrace. She thought he was going to hold her, comfort her poor smarting behind, but then nothing he'd done this evening had been precisely what she'd expected. With a little adjusting, he spread the fly of his jeans, releasing his hard-on. Angie didn't have to be told what to do next. She lifted her hips and then slipped down on his cock, feeling all the stinging pain in her backside concentrate to a pulsing throb, enhancing this delicious moment of pleasure.

Todd gripped her hips through the silky fabric of her patterned dress, working her up and down on his cock. She held his gaze with her own, feeling the wetness on her tear-stained cheeks, feeling the rush of the impending orgasm wing through her. Her ass felt on fire as he continued to fuck her, but there was no denying that the spanking had made her the most turned on of her life. She and Todd had shared exciting sex previously—out on the balcony, up in the hills against his car—but nothing like this. This was brand-new, the best she'd ever had.

When Todd pressed his fingers between their bodies, stroking her clit, she came. She kept her eyes on his as the pleasure flowed through her, and he bucked his hips once more, coming a beat later, filling her.

"No more lying," she promised Todd, looking meekly into his eyes.

"Good girl," he said, nodding. "Because spankings don't have to wait for birthdays."

She grinned at him, knowing suddenly that it didn't matter—the numbers didn't matter. And knowing for certain that she was never going to be twenty-nine again.

FORTY-SEVEN CANDLES

Sage Vivant

One month earlier, he'd asked her to dinner for this evening.

"I want mine to be the first birthday invitation you get," he said as they stopped to chat between cases at the courthouse.

She raised an eyebrow, considering him and his suggestion. "I accept on one condition," she grinned.

"Always a contingency clause. What is it?"

"If some young stud asks me between now and then, I get to go with him. I only like men half my age, as you know."

He chuckled and shook his head. "Sally, I'm afraid no one could ever accuse you of hypocrisy. I always know where I stand with you!"

"Oh, Gerry! You know how dear you are to me!" Alarm crossed her face with charming authenticity. She obviously hadn't meant to hurt his feelings. She placed a hand on his arm imploringly.

"I'd love to have dinner with you on my birthday," she smiled, looking directly into his face. They'd both been on their way to a hearing where Sally worked as his court reporter, so there wasn't much time for further discussion.

He phoned her a couple of days before her birthday to confirm their date.

"Have I been ousted by some well-hung man-child?" he joked.

She laughed and told him not only was the date still on, but she was looking forward to it.

As he drove up to her house, he interpreted the available parking space as a promising omen and pulled in quickly. He almost regretted having to leave it to go to dinner.

Words eluded him briefly when she opened her door to greet him. He'd seen her dressed up a few times before, and certainly, she always presented a chic, attractive package in arbitration hearings, but this was different. Lit from the interior lights behind her and the moon from above, she was half apparition, half woman.

"Hello," she smiled, enjoying his momentary discomfiture.

"You look stunning," he finally managed.

"Thank you," she replied with an endearing mix of confidence and relief. Her coat was on her arm and she didn't invite him in. Just as well, he thought. She looked much too fetching to be alone with.

"Shall we go?" she asked, stepping out and closing the door behind her. They were on their way to Hawthorne Lane in minutes.

Over impeccably prepared meals, they shared arbitration gossip and slowly relaxed. He never forgot how delicious she looked but at least by the time dessert menus arrived, he was less obsessed with her appearance.

They were sharing an elaborate chocolate concoction when she turned suddenly serious.

"I just want you to know, Gerry, that I was so touched by your invitation. You're such a good friend to me."

He picked up his wineglass and she mirrored him. "To being forty-seven. May this be the year you find true love." Glasses clinked.

"An overrated state of being. Better I should find true lust!" Her eyes sparkled.

"Well, I've offered..."

"To find me true lust?"

"To provide it."

"No, you want to provide love *and* lust. Love is complicated and confusing. And all that worry about who's cheating on who! With lust, things are simple. You satisfy a primal urge, affirm your sexuality, and get on with life. Really young men function on that premise and look at them. So full of life and energy. That's what I want, not some stodgy, quiet existence with the same aging guy for years and years."

He stared at her a moment, absorbing her remark. "Couldn't I just get a blow job?"

She laughed so hard she blushed. Finally, she spoke. "That's against your principles, as I recall."

"Do I have principles?"

"Oh, stop it. Aren't you the guy who thinks sex should only happen when love is present?"

"Yes, but thanks to William Jefferson Clinton, there's a new definition of sex. I'm willing to consider that new definition. After all, it sets a legal precedent."

"You're impossible," she laughed.

"I take it the answer is no, then," he persisted.

"Eat your chocolate."

He sighed melodramatically to amuse her but the defeat still stung.

She invited him in when they returned to her house. Unfortunately, they had to park two blocks away. The night was cooler now, windy too, and the couple walked briskly toward her house.

A moving van sat curbside. When she saw it, she stopped walking and grabbed his arm.

"Gerry!" she hissed. "Look! A van!"

He wondered what on earth was in her head. It was just a van, for god's sake.

"Yes...."

"Haven't you heard stories about burglars who pretend they're moving or making a delivery so they look legit and then they clean you out of everything you own?" She wouldn't move. He happily used her distress as an excuse to put his arm around her. Her firm curves felt even better than they looked.

"Sal, there's no activity. Probably somebody's going to use the van in the morning."

"Sure, there's no activity now! They're already in my house, scoping out what they want. Oh, use your cell phone to call the police!" she urged.

He stroked her arm to soothe her. "Why don't you just let me go in and check things out? The cops won't come with the evidence we've got so far, anyway. Give me your key."

She hesitated. She didn't want him risking his life for the sake of her possessions. He assured her the risk was minimal and went inside.

He walked through her house, turning on lights as he went, pausing at her bedroom before moving on. In minutes, he returned to the sidewalk and motioned her inside.

"You did that awfully quickly. Are you sure there's nobody in there?"

Holding her hand, he led her through each room until she was convinced they were alone. He poured them each a drink.

"You see, this is a perfect example of how useful it could be to have a true love around," he commented.

She took a swig from the glass he proffered. "Uh-huh," she said flatly, collapsing into the corner of her sofa. "But you must admit it's strange that a van should be there at this hour."

"I think you think too much. I'm sure there's a good explanation."

"Oh, sure. Give me one."

"Maybe that's where all your birthday candles are being stored."

She grabbed a pillow and flung it at him. At least she laughed.

"Try again," she said.

"I'm serious," he insisted, taking the cell phone she had insisted he purchase out of his breast pocket. He dialed and then spoke into the phone.

"Okay, it's time for those forty-seven candles to come out."

"Very funny. Your evasive tactics may work in the courtroom but not with me!"

The doorbell rang. Panic consumed her face and she locked gazes with him. "Who could that be?"

"I'll get it." He moved toward the door.

She leapt up to stop him, but it was too late. He not only had the door open but was ushering a man inside. Out of the corner of his eye, he saw her step back, as each man passed through the threshold.

"Gerry—"

Smiling, he made his way through the crowd of young,

handsome men in dark trench coats. She looked frightened but gradually noticed how attractive her uninvited guests were. Her face softened.

"What's going on?" she demanded, grinning.

"These are the forty-seven candles I was telling you about. And each one of them is half your age: twenty-three and a half. Isn't that right, boys?"

A resounding cheer rose up en masse. She giggled, guffawed, then reddened.

"I'm not sure I understand," she ventured.

"Show her, gentlemen."

All forty-seven dropped their coats to the floor, revealing a sea of muscled chests and six-pack abs. All of them were naked save for tiny little Speedos that cradled their impressive privates.

"Are they going to dance for me?" She was still red.

"They'll do whatever you like. It's *your* birthday. But I don't think I'd waste their time with music," he said, kissing her on the cheek. "I'm going to let you enjoy your gift in private." He walked out, shutting the door behind him.

He remained on the stairs, debating. Should he go back in and make sure she was safe? Or should he just watch from a window? Neither would be gentlemanly. He headed toward his car, letting his erection lead the way.

Once he had made his way to the car, he couldn't bring himself to go home. Instead, he drove the two blocks back to Sally's house, praying for better parking. There was none. He was suddenly obsessed with the notion of keeping vigil, of knowing exactly when all forty-seven of those raging hard-ons left her house. He sidled up to a driveway across the street and parked there, blocking access. He could always move if somebody needed to come or go.

He looked at the house longingly. He pulled his zipper down, aware that his list of offenses was growing. First a parking violation for blocking a driveway, and now he was heading into indecent exposure. He didn't care. The thought of Sally with all those studs disrupted his logical mind like some electrical charge, deconstructing his thoughts into monosyllabic noises and primal compulsions.

One of the men steps toward her, sensing her excitement but needing to quell her anxiety. He leans his face into hers to kiss her. The warmth of his smooth, naked skin dizzies her as his lips nip at hers softly. She likes his aura; his touch is welcoming. She responds by parting her lips and searching for his tongue. The man caresses her neck and kisses her passionately.

She gets wet almost immediately. The other men undress her gently. She allows it and continues kissing the first man. The zipper of her dress runs down the length of her back. Hands at her shoulders slip the dress over her arms and past her hips until it puddles at her feet.

Big, strong hands roam over her warm skin. Some of the men comment.

"Mmmm, nice ass."

"Oh, yeah, this is gonna be fun."

"Are you getting wet, baby?"

She flushes at the attention and moves now to the mouth of another young stud. Deft fingers unhook her bra. It's off her in seconds and her freed breasts liberate her libido further. Her body gets hotter as many hands grope at her breasts.

A couple of men stoop a bit to take her nipples into their mouths. She groans as they suck and lick at her. Meanwhile, other hands squeeze and jiggle her breasts. Her head reels with all the attention lavished on her tits!

But there's more work to be done. Many busy hands at her smooth, shapely thighs unsnap garters from nylon. Palms push the stockings down her legs, running along her calves sensually.

Several men slip her stockings and shoes off her. She stands there, in the middle of her living room, naked and steamy, making out at random with hungry, anonymous mouths of twenty-three-and-a-half-year-old men.

The men peel off their Speedos, not in unison because that would look rehearsed. Rather they do it when it strikes them. All of them closest to Sally strip within seconds of each other.

Every single cock reads twelve o'clock and is as hard as any other muscle on the men's bodies. Six or seven men press their enormous, solid cocks against her hips and thighs. There's a cock between her asscheeks, one at each flank, one tickling her pussy hair. There are more but she's aware of mostly these.

One of the strapping young bucks suddenly picks her up, like she was his bride. He looks into her eyes with an expression meant to make her swoon with anticipation. It fulfills its promise.

"Where's your bedroom?" Adonis asks her.

She directs him and his forty-six pals to her boudoir, but wonders aloud, "I don't know if there's room for all of you!"

The men laugh at her naivete and swarm to her room.

She is placed on her bed, face up. The perfect male specimens surround her, a human fence soon to protect her from absolutely nothing. She watches them with their hard, flat stomachs; chiseled muscles; long, thick cocks raring for pussy. Her pussy! She is suddenly struck by the prospect of accommodating every penis in the room and shuts her eyes to keep her fear from showing.

Lips touch her arms and legs. Tongues swirl around her nipples. It's an oral orgy. Strong hands grasp her ankles and spread her legs wide open. Fingers frig her swollen clit while others dip into her juicy opening. Still others just spread her cream around. Someone French-kisses her just as a tongue slides into her slit. When another tongue flicks at her clit, she squeals but the sound is muffled in the head of her kissing lover.

She cannot collect her thoughts to count the number of men on her bed administering pleasure to her body. Her pussy has never been so wet. It seems to be working overtime to be sure every man gets enough.

There are tongues between the folds of her cunt, tongues along the insides of her thighs. Mouths on her tits, sucking, endlessly sucking her nipples. She feels swollen beyond reversal and ready to explode.

She realizes she needs cock to balance these sensations. Looking about her furtively, she tries to focus on nearby members she can grab. But the search is difficult not only because there are so many moving bodies but also because one cock looks better than the next. She can't choose among them! Finally, she takes hold of those nearest. With one in each hand, she is surprised at her next words.

"Somebody fuck me!"

A man with a particularly tight, round butt straddles her face. He guides his big dick into her mouth—she can't assist because her hands are busy pumping cock. The man on her face feeds her his cock, sliding in and out of her slowly like she needs to get used to the idea. His pace heightens the eroticism of his movements and she writhes impatiently.

She cannot see past her mouth-fucker but she's aware that there's no longer a finger inside her. Instead, a cock of astounding proportions pushes itself so deeply into her dripping snatch that it seems destined to drill a hole right through to her mattress. Despite the cocks in her mouth and pussy, she does not let go of the ones in her hands.

A new cock replaces the one in her pussy and pumps her hard, shaking the bed. She feels wetter and wonders if each man is coming inside her. She feels only the desire to be fucked again and again.

Several more pricks make their way up her juicy hole. Her delirium has long since taken over and she doesn't even know if she's conscious.

Dozens of hands lift her up and turn her on her stomach. Somebody pulls her ass up, bringing her to the doggie position. Hands are all over her body now—her back, her stomach, her legs. Men position themselves under her breasts like hungry farm animals.

She runs a hand over the perfect stomachs of three men and smiles, unwilling yet to believe so many young, beautiful men are servicing her.

A raven-haired stud kneels before her and guides her head to his waiting meat. She gobbles him up noisily. The men at her breasts increase their noise level, sucking and licking audibly.

The action between her legs is incredible. Somebody's tongue rims her asshole while her hard clit is expertly fondled. A huge cock rams into her cunt so hard her asscheeks jiggle. She feels her brain bouncing off the walls, feels her muscles tighten, and then when she cannot contain the onslaught of pleasure anymore, her entire body undulates and heaves with release.

She orgasms over and over, unable to stop. The cock in her sopping wet pussy just keeps pumping and whatever it is at her clit relentless strokes her. Eventually, perhaps when all the men are empty, the fucking and frigging and sucking and licking draw to a close.

She collapses on her stomach. Big, strong hands caress her backside and voices urge her to sleep.

Gerry wondered how much longer the forty-seven candles would need to satisfy Sally. What were they doing? What was she doing? How long would it take for forty-seven men to please one woman? Could he stand to wait and find out?

He had stayed this long; he could stay a little longer. His curiosity consumed him.

Ten minutes later, her front door opened and every trench-coated god emerged. They returned to the moving van with admirable stealth and speed. But was Sally satisfied?

His phone rang, jarring him.

"Gerry," she said dreamily. So this is what she sounded like freshly laid.

"Hi, baby. Did you enjoy your birthday present?"

"It was *sooooo* incredible. I may not walk for days!"

"That's good."

"But I just want you to know," she drawled into the phone, still oozing sex, "I want to do something nice for you to show my gratitude."

"You do, do you? What do you want to do?" This was it. This had to be it.

"I'd like to give you that blow job," she giggled languidly.

"Would you like me to come in now?" he purred.

"No, no, I'm wiped out. But really, Gerry, before you die, I promise to suck you off."

"Before I die?"

"Yes, I promise. And thank you again for my candles!" After several clicks and some rustling, the connection was severed.

He looked at the phone, like people do in the movies.

"Before I die. Well, *vive la* Gerry!" he mumbled wryly.

He pointed his car toward home.

ANOTHER TEN FOR EXTRA

Erica Dumas

M eet me at eleven," I told you. "Twelve-two-twenty-seven, Route thirty-four. Bring five hundred dollars in cash, and don't make any excuses. You'll need it."

Did you look up the address on the Web, or did you just trust me? I worry about it for most of the evening, but when stage time approaches I have about a million other things to worry about. Like the fact, just for instance, that my breasts keep popping out of the little black bikini, that the two days of wearing the six-inch heels have given me blisters, and—most important of all—the club is packed, shoulder to shoulder and chair to chair, unbelievable, one of the other dancers tells me, even on a Saturday night with the amateur winners.

Saturday is when they debut the new dancers, which is why I've got my chance; it's not amateur tryouts, which I did on Tuesday, or amateur finals, which I did on Thursday. I didn't tell you about either one of those, for a very simple reason: Amateurs don't give lap dances. I made it through both rounds and landed one of the three coveted spots as a house dancer, and tonight's my debut. After my time on the stage, I'll slip backstage and then ease my way into the crowd, finding the guy who wants me to give him my very first lap dance. I wouldn't want that to be anyone but you.

It's a birthday present, after all. It's only once a year I get a chance to really, truly blow your mind. I think this night will do it.

They call my name and I ease onto the stage as my song begins to play—it's *our* song, one of our favorite songs to fuck to, something that makes me want sex acutely the instant I hear its opening throb. I press myself up against the stripper pole, expecting it to be cold, finding it warm. Warm from the last dancer. Kendra was her name, or something like it, and she whipped the crowd into a frenzy. Even now she's headed into the crowd to give her first round of lap dances. The same place I'll be going in a few minutes. But before I can get there, I have to knock 'em dead.

And I know I'm going to, from the first moment I mount the brass pole and show them the Snake, inverting myself high on the pole and sliding gradually down, hanging on with both hands and spreading my legs. The crowd's going wild, and five-dollar bills are laid out on the edge of the stage, waiting for me to take them.

I crawl over, heart pounding as I look into the lights and hope that you're there. What if you're late? What if you miss the whole performance? What if some other guy grabs me and wants a lap dance? I can't care. I *won't* care. I have to be what I've come here to be: a stripper, a birthday-present stripper for you.

I wriggle my way across the stage, undulating with splayed thighs as the cheers grow in volume. I pick up one bill in my mouth, rub another over my breasts before tucking it in. Then I inch my knees forward to the edge of the stage, spread my legs and lean far, far back because I see a dark-haired man holding a twenty.

The lights are so bright, I don't recognize you; I know you're going to think this is crazy, but I only realize it's you, at first, because I *smell* you. I can't explain it. Even over the stink of the club—the cigarettes, booze, and male sweat—I know your scent mingled up in it all. When your hand slides down into my G-string, depositing the twenty-dollar bill, I know I'm pushing the rules, but I let you linger a little while before pulling back. Did you know what I was planning all along? It doesn't much matter, because I'm leaning forward, over the edge of the stage, reaching out to caress your face and your eyes stare into mine, hunger amped up with an intensity I've almost never seen in them. I lick my lips, allowing my tongue to laze in a slow circle. There's another twenty in your hand. The first rubs against my clit. As I lean forward, your fingers bend the rules again, lingering too long, and this bill finds one of my nipples. Prickly at first, then smooth, it feels delicious.

I move back from the stage and mount the pole again, spinning right side up and then upside down, working my top until it gently peels open of its own accord and falls away. I can't see you—you're lost in the spots—but I aim for you, a good toss and I pray you catch it. Then I'm fully inverted, legs spread wide, and I wonder how much the other men can see. They're hooting in approval of my breasts, which are all natural, a rarity, even for the amateur winners. After a few more spins and a crawl across the stage, I'm ready for more tips. I wish each one was from you, but we can't have everything. Patrons are grumbling when I make my way across the stage—you're one of those guys who fixates on a dancer, proffering twenties like candy, never giving the other patrons their chance. I lean way back and the bills nudge my clit. My G-string is stuffed with your money, now. And I'm about to use it.

Once I lose the bottoms, once I go full nude, I can't hit the edge of the stage; I can't let the patrons give me tips. It doesn't matter, though, because what I've been aching for is not just the feeling of your money tucked into my skimpy clothes, but even more so the feeling of exhilaration as I gently tug the ties at the sides of my G-string, as I expose myself in front of all these men, in full view of you—everyone seeing what only you're going to get. I stretch out on the stage, arch my back, and gently slide the G-string out from between my spread legs, positioning myself so I'm sure you can see everything.

I know you well enough to know you've got a hard-on in your pants, and that thought alone would be enough to make my smooth-shaven pussy, spread wide for the howling crowd, glisten with drizzling moisture—if it wasn't already.

The song ends, the announcer says my stage name—and the crowd erupts in applause. I take a slow saunter around the stage, plucking up bills, some of them moist with my juices, the others moist with my sweat—and theirs. I disappear through the black curtain to another round of applause. Despite the six-inch heels, I practically sprint for the dressing room.

Now it's time for the main event—well, not quite. First I need to thread my way through the club, avoiding the eyes of the men who hold up bills, indiscreetly trying to show me that they're twenties—the going rate for a lap dance. I ignore them and make my way through the crowd looking for one guy—and I find him, near the back away from the action where you've probably tipped the bouncer to get access to one of the curtained enclosures.

After I spot you I see two different girls make their moves

on you, seeing the fanned bills on your knee. You wave both of them off with the same casual indifference with which I ignore the patrons trying to flag me down. You're tucked back into the cubicle, relaxing on the little red velvet couch. Even in the shadows, I can see your hard cock tenting your pants. It's all I can do not to pounce on you right then and there, take your zipper down and ease your cock into my mouth. It takes all of my restraint just to cock one hip toward you, watching your eyes slide sensuously from the tops of my shoes to the hem of my skintight plaid schoolgirl skirt, up the curves of my belly to the loosely tied halter that shrouds my breasts—nipples showing through the formfitting material, obvious even in the dim light—then to my face, made up like a whore's, haloed as it is by teased bleach-blonde hair.

Till now I've never bleached my hair, never shaved my pussy. I've never danced in front of a room full of howling men—or planned the sort of thing I can't chicken out of now. I thought I could keep the hunger under control, but the moment I see you I'm wet to the knees, and I don't know how the hell I'm going to keep us from getting thrown out of here.

"Could I interest you in a lap dance, sir?"

You've got a scotch in one hand; you sip it. With your other hand you hold up the twenties—five of them. "How much?"

I react like a regular stripper at the sight of the money—I make my way around the little table, as gracefully as I can in six-inch heels. I slide into the tiny couch, take my place up close to you.

"Table dance or lap dance?" I ask.

"What's the difference?" you ask me, caressing my cleavage with the smooth money.

"For a table dance, I get fully nude," I say, leaning close to you—kissing is forbidden, and when you bring your lips toward mine I pull back, shivering. There are curtains on three sides, but the bouncers can see in if they want to. The heat of it makes me so fucking wet I feel like every cell in my body is humming with my need to fuck your brains out—right here, right now. I open my mouth to speak, but my voice catches in my throat. I can feel my stomach churning, the heat in my clit is so powerful that I can't even go on playing the game. I just freeze up, choking.

"Fully nude?" you say.

"Uh-huh," I nod.

"Do you hide anything?"

I shake my head. "Not a thing."

"And why wouldn't I want a beautiful girl like you nude?" you ask me.

"I have to stay on the table," I say.

"Well, I certainly don't want that," you say.

"With a lap dance," I finally manage to whimper, "the G-string stays on."

"But you're in my lap." Your lips move closer to mine.

I nod slightly. "But I'm in your lap." I meant to just say it softly, but it comes out as the faintest kind of whimpers.

Your eyes are locked on mine. I can smell your breath; the scent of scotch on it always turns me on.

"My lap's very nice," you tell me.

"Twenty for one song," I answer. "Another ten for an extra."

"What's an extra?" you ask me, the smirk on your face telling me exactly what you're asking.

I shiver slightly.

"An extra song," I tell you.

"I thought you meant something else," you tell me. "How much for that?" Your eyes drop from my face to my breasts to the hem of my plaid skirt. I've never seen you wanting me so bad. I've never seen you so savage in your hunger, like you would give anything, do anything, to fuck me right here before the bouncers could stop us.

I open my mouth to answer, but my voice catches in my throat.

"We don't do that here," I say breathlessly, my clit so firm against the G-string that it almost hurts me to move. "We don't do that."

You respond with a smug little smile.

"But if you did," you tell me, "I bet it would cost a lot."

You reach into your suit jacket, pull out a black wallet, take out every bill in there. There's more than the five hundred I told you to bring. These bills are hundreds. Maybe a dozen of them. Maybe more. You stack them neatly with the other five. You pluck away the top of my halter, slip all the bills into it just as a new song begins. It's some slow-grind heavy metal ballad, annoying and bluesy; normally I could never dance to this. But I'm on you in an instant, spread over your lap, feeling the pulse of your hard cock pressing against my thigh before I can even tell you what I'm supposed to tell you. Your hands are on my ass, going up my skirt, ready to feel how wet I am—and I would give almost anything to not have to tell you to stop. But that's not the fantasy. That's not the game.

"No hands," I say firmly. "You've got to put them flat on the couch."

"Or what?" you growl, your finger sliding between my thighs and nuzzling its way under my G-string. You bring a gasp and a long, low moan from my lips, and I lean in close.

"Or those nice bouncers beat you up," I say, and arch my back, pushing slightly away from you.

Your hands head to the couch, and I glance over my shoulder to make sure no one's noticed. Before you plant your right hand, I reach down, grasp the wrist, bring your hand up to my face.

I kiss your middle finger, tasting my sex, my eyes languid as I watch you watching me, my tongue swirling around your fingertip. I taste good.

I release your wrist, let you plant your hand obediently, and begin my slow grind atop you, legs spread, facing you.

"How long have you had this job?" you ask me hoarsely as I work my hips and wriggle my upper body in time with the music.

"Tonight's my first night," I tell you. "You're my first customer."

"Your first lap-dance customer," you breathe.

I nod as I arch my back and run a shimmy from ass to breasts, jiggling slightly.

"You're very good at it," you say.

I lean close, my brightly painted lips close to your ear as the metal song oozes slowly into electronica. "You have no idea," I whisper, and tug the loose knot out of my halter. "But you're about to find out."

Your eyes widen as I peel away the sweaty material. As I do, I quickly palm the stack of bills and slip it into the waistband of my skirt, feeling it electric against my flesh. My nipples quickly cool in the air-conditioning, getting even more erect than before, and you lean forward to touch one with your tongue.

"Uh-uh," I whimper softly. You look up at me, frustrated and titillated at the same time. I ease my body back and forth, dancing in front of you, holding my breasts just out of your reach. You take a drink of scotch. You try again, lips parted, eyes locked with mine, your mouth reaching within half an inch of my nipple before I shake my head and sway back from you, taking my breasts out of your reach. I come up fast and cradle your head, your breath scotch-sweet in my face. Your hand comes off the sofa and I don't know how you got the twenty in your hand, but it's there—I know it; I can feel it against my flesh as you slip it into my waistband. I glance over my shoulder and see no one's watching. I lean closer. Your mouth closes over my nipple. Your scotch is on the rocks and I gasp as you press the ice against me. I whimper softly and grind up and down on you, feeling your hard-on rubbing against my clit. I'm aching. I want you so bad, I simply can't stand it.

The ice starts to melt in your mouth, and you crunch and then swallow it, relinquishing the taste of my nipple. As I lean back and work my hips, your hand disappears into the pocket of your coat and comes out holding another roll of bills. The sight of it makes my stomach swirl.

I lean close. "What do you think that'll get you?" I ask you.

"You tell me," comes your reply, and your lips take mine, suckling hungrily as your tongue enters my mouth.

I can't take it anymore. I can't fucking take it anymore. Every rule is about to be broken—and I don't care. I perform a quick twirl over you, reversing my position, planting myself with one six-inch heel on either side of your wing tips, my fingers loosening the buckles of my schoolgirl skirt—not so I can take it off, but because I need it to hang low for camouflage.

There's a new song starting as I tug the hem of my skirt down.

I glance up, back and forth, all around, looking for bouncers, looking for customers taking too close an interest. Looking for other dancers eager to get one of the new girls fired. There's no one—as busy as it is, patrons, bouncers, and dancers are all occupied with their individual tasks. We're safe—for now.

I look down at you over my shoulder and talk to you as softly as I can while being sure that you'll hear me—we can't afford to dawdle.

"Take it out," I tell you, and your widening eyes tell me you've heard.

I block the sight of your hands from the rest of the club. You make short work of your belt and zipper; I know it's out and ready because you put your hands flat on the sofa again.

With one fluid motion, I reach back, pull up the back of my skirt, and pluck my G-string to one side. Then I find the tip of your cock with my finger, guide it between my shaved lips, and sit down on it as casually as a girl can fuck herself onto a cock she's dreamed about all night.

I have to stifle a moan, because it feels so fucking good to have your cock sliding deep inside me, entering me from behind, in a position that always drives me crazy. I can feel the thick head of your naked cock grinding against my G-spot, and I swear my eyes cross so bad I can't even keep an eye out for the bouncers. I come to my senses an instant later as the pleasure settles down to a dull roar, and I open my mouth wide to moan, only barely stopping myself by shaking my head to clear it.

"Hands on the sofa," I tell you firmly as I feel your fingertips begin to creep up my belly toward my breasts. It's the first time I've been firm with you. I can't afford to have the bouncers watch me now. Not with what I'm doing. Not with what I'm *about* to do.

I sit down firmly in your lap, lean forward both to more effectively hide what we're doing and to drive you up harder and deeper into me. I rock back and forth and bite my lip to keep from screaming. Your hands are on me and I have to grab and remove them—but not before you've managed to get a grip on my breasts and pinch my nipples, which feels so fucking good that it drives me toward my orgasm even faster than I was already going. I open my eyes wide, looking around desperately and hoping no one's seen—then my vision goes white and my head starts to spin, as I pulse toward climax and work my hips more eagerly, fucking myself harder onto your cock. My orgasm explodes deep inside me, more intense than any you've given me yet—pleasure that splits me in two, popping my mouth open wide and making me want to scream. Then I can feel you coming, the wetness spurting deep inside me, a sensation as familiar as it is exciting, and my orgasm soars higher as I struggle to catch my breath. You don't make a sound—or at least nothing I can hear over the music—which is more than I can say for me, even as I struggle to keep my mouth shut. My moan draws a few quick glances—and as I finish myself off on your cock, I know my days as a semiprofessional stripper are over.

I lean back in your lap, feeling your cock pop out of me underneath the plaid skirt. I reach back and caress your face. I kiss you, deeply, tasting scotch and the salt of my sweat.

"Happy birthday," you tell me.

"You were an awfully good sport about it," I say.

"How could I not be?" You chuckle. "Was it as good as the fantasy?"

"Better," I whisper. "Much better. But I think it's about to be over."

One of the bouncers is watching us, eyes narrowed to slits.

"There a back door in this place?"

I giggle softly, brush my fingertips across your cheek, and kiss you.

"Yes, there's a back door," I whisper. "But that'll have to wait until we get home."

"Then what are we waiting for?"

I wriggle back into my halter top and leave the sweatpants, tank top and flip-flops in my locker backstage. The bouncer gives me a bewildered look as I lead you out the back door.

SANDRA BOISE TURNS THIRTY

Michael Hemmingson

A.

Ah, my friend Sandra Boise's birthday is tomorrow. She is turning thirty and not happy about it.

"My thirtieth was great," I tell her while we are at the bar and getting drunk. "I was living with this woman, Terrah, and dating another woman, a married woman, her name was Irene."

"Wait," says Sandra, "you were seeing a married woman?"

"It was cool."

"Maybe for the two of you, but what about her husband and your girlfriend?"

"Her husband didn't know, and Terrah and I had an understanding."

"Oh, an 'understanding.' Uh-huh."

Now I get annoyed: "Would you *let* me tell my story?"

She rolls her eyes. "Tell."

"Terrah was bi, so I could fool around with other women as long as she could have sex with them too," I say. I'm sure my voice sounds nostalgic with the fine memories of sexual encounters from the past. "Irene didn't care for having lesbian experiences, so she had no interest in Terrah. This was bugging Terrah; she felt like I was having an affair. She felt left out. I told Irene this. Terrah threw me a huge birthday bash when I turned thirty. Irene wanted to make it special. At the party she said she was ready. 'Ready for what?' I said. She said she was ready to have sex with Terrah; she would do this as a birthday present. I was like, 'Yeah!' "

"I bet you were."

"I thought it was the best birthday present ever."

"You were *excited.*"

"I got hard just listening to her words. Irene wanted to get naked right there in the middle of the party. We just needed to find Terrah. We found her in the bedroom. Perfect place, right? But she was drunk."

"Like us?"

"We're not drunk yet."

"Getting there," Sandra says, and waves at the bartender for another round.

"The problem with Terrah," I tell her, "she was passed out."

"She was that drunk."

"Yeah. We tried to wake her up—"

"To have sex?"

"That's what we were there for. Listen, Boise, are you going to let me tell my story or not?"

"Am I interrupting?"

"Aren't you always?"

"So I'll keep my mouth shut," she says. "Where were you? Oh yeah, you and Irene were gonna fuck Terrah but Terrah was passed out."

"Needless to say," I say, "I was greatly disappointed. But Irene was getting undressed. So I pulled off all of Terrah's clothes."

Sandra is about to say something but stops herself.

"Yes," I say, "Terrah was asleep but I wanted her naked. Just in case she woke up. So Irene and I get on the bed and we have sex next to Terrah's body. Then we have sex on her body. It was hot. I came on Terrah's skin and Irene and I rubbed it all over her. That was my thirtieth birthday."

B.

Booze. After a couple more drinks, Sandra Boise says, "I have a kinky birthday tale. Let me tell it and you better not interrupt me, motherfucker, because you know how I like my running, rambling monologues, and this is one: I'm twenty-one, I'm twenty and about to turn twenty-one, and I've been dating this guy, this older guy (by older I mean he's like twenty-five; okay, I'm lying, he's thirty-five, okay?) and so he says to me: 'So what do you want for b-day twenty-one? Go out to a bar and get shit-faced drunk?' and I say: 'No, what I would like for my birthday is to fuck you in the ass with a strap-on.' He takes a pregnant pause (I like that phrase) and he goes: 'Are you serious?' I tell him of course I'm serious and he says why and I tell him because ever since I was a bat out of high school I've had fantasies of fucking men with strap-ons. 'Look,' I say, 'you like me to lick your asshole, so I bet you'd like me to fuck your asshole.' 'Look,' he says, 'I fuck you there, you don't fuck me there.' 'Look,' I say, 'this is my birthday wish, okay?' 'Okay,' he says.... Later...after I lick his asshole real good, after I get my nose and tongue up there, he says, 'You can have your birthday present.' So next week my birthday arrives and I have bought this especially big strap-on dildo to fuck him with and I didn't expect him to like it. You want to know the truth? I wanted to hurt him. I wanted to hurt him because I didn't really like him, he was too old for me, and I thought maybe this would be a good way to get rid of him. I'd have some fun, he'd be ashamed, or angry, and that would be that. But no, that is not what happened. You wanna know what happened? The guy loved it. He screamed with joy. He said I opened him up to new possibilities, he said I made his soul soar, he said I showed him his true self with that fake dick up his ass and he wanted me to fuck him all the time. All the time. So I did. And I got bored with it. So I dumped him. He was very depressed."

C.

Cab. We're taking a taxi, Sandra Boise and I, because we're now too damn drunk to drive. We leave the bar. We take a cab. I guess we're going back to her place. In the cab, she reaches over and grabs my crotch. She says, "Yum. Yum. And yum?"

"What?"

"I'm *in the mood.*"

"How rare."

"We're just friends," she says, moving her hand away.

I grab her hand and put it back.

"Oh?" she says.

"Friendly friends," I say.

That old Bauhaus song runs through my mind, "A Spy in the Cab."

D.

"Dick, I love dick," says Sandra Boise, and gives me a blow job the first thing after we step inside her studio apartment. It's a cramped place and she has a Murphy bed.

E.

"Eat my pussy," she says fifteen minutes later, naked on her Murphy bed, pushing my head into her crotch, "eat that kitty and eat it long and good, fucker...."

F.

"Feet," she sighs an hour later. "Lick my feet, suck my toes," and she puts her right foot up to my mouth. "You into feet fetish stuff?"

"No."

"You are now."

"Yes," I say, and put her big toe in my mouth.

G.

"Get on your knees," I tell her.

Sandra Boise is in the bathtub. I hold my placid cock. She closes her eyes. I start to pee on her.

H.

"Happy birthday," I tell her as we take a shower together, getting sober.

"I'm not thirty yet," she says softly. "Tomorrow, yes. But not today."

I.

"I want a special birthday present from you," says Sandra Boise after the shower. We dry each other off with one dirty towel.

"To fuck me in the ass with a strap-on?" I say. "Sure, you can do that. I can get into that."

"I have a different unfulfilled fantasy," she says.

"Yeah?"

"Yeah. I want to menstruate on a man."

"What?"

"Call it a bloody shower. Not golden, not brown, but red."

"You've done this before?"

"No. No, you idiot, that's why I want it for a birthday present. I've been thinking about it for years. No guy I've dated would do it. I can't even get guys to fuck me when I'm on my period."

"Why not? Warm and squishy."

"See, I knew you'd be into it. Because you're a pervert."

J.

I jack off on her birthday, while on my back, legs up, as Sandra Boise fucks me with her strap-on dick. I like it but she's bored. She's thirty now.

K.

"Okay," Sandra Boise says, "I'm ready now."

It's a week later. I'm lying naked on her bathroom floor. She's naked and squatting over me. She's on her period. Her flow flows slowly like a lost dream onto my skin. She moves up and down my body, the blood like a line of ink. She moves her pussy over my face. I taste her and she tastes like something from my distant childhood that I can't determine.

She looks down at me, at the blood. She rubs it into my skin, like I rubbed my semen into Terrah's flesh that birthday night long ago.

"Why?" I ask.

"Because it's so dirty," she says.

L.

"I love you," she says before I leave. "Now."

CHASING HER DREAM

Michelle Houston

Lydia pulled the top off her second pint of Häagen-Dazs, and dug her spoon in. After licking the delicious coffee ice cream from the underside of the spoon, she slid the spoon into her mouth and moaned softly. Although she wasn't feeling much better, the sugar rush was helping some. She hated feeling depressed on her birthday. Depressed—and dumped only made it that much worse.

A hard pounding on her front door drew her attention away from her comfort food. She sat there and listened to the sound of a fist hitting wood, completely unwilling to get up and see who it was.

"Lydia, open the door, damn it!"

Oh great, she thought, *just what I need. Good guy Shawn coming to my rescue.* Shawn, who she had been lusting over since before she started dating the loser. "Go away!"

"Not until I make sure that you're all right."

Grimacing, she set down her ice cream and headed to the

door, pausing along the way to pull her robe on over her pajamas. Unlocking it, she swung the door open and confronted her unwanted savior. "I'm alive. You happy now?"

"Nope." In a move typical of his take-charge behavior, Shawn shouldered past her into the living room. Lydia watched in shock as he plopped down onto her sofa and picked up her ice cream. "Coffee. My favorite."

It was him dipping her spoon into her ice cream that drew Lydia out of her stupor. "That's mine!" she snarled as she yanked it from his hands. Shawn let the ice cream go only to clasp her hips in his large hands and pull her into his lap.

"There, now that I've got your attention, tell me what happened."

Lydia struggled to get up, but weakened by a day of crying, she soon gave up and settled into the warmth and comfort her friend offered. "He broke up with me."

"I know that part. He told me at the gym. When he told me that he left you crying, and laughed about it, I hit him."

"He laughed about it?" If anything, it made her feel worse. Struggling to hold back the fresh tears, she scooped another spoonful of ice cream up and licked it off the spoon.

"Sorry, I shouldn't have told you that." Shawn pulled the ice cream from her hands and set it aside before he continued. "It made him feel like a big man or something. Although all of the guys were fairly pissed at him, and I know if I hadn't, several of them would have hit him themselves."

"I'm glad you hit him," she mumbled against his chest as she burrowed into his warmth. Although her relationship had just ended, it wasn't the fact that it was over that hurt, it was how much she had misjudged her ex. She knew she would get over him, but wasn't sure how long it would take her to trust a new guy.

"So, what happened?"

Shawn's warm hand clasped the back of her neck, tipping her head to the side, then he ran his fingers through her hair. She wanted to melt into him, it felt so good.

"We had a fight. He called me a sexual deviant and told me he wanted nothing to do with me."

"You? A sexual deviant?" Lydia could feel the rumble of his laughter deep in his chest. "You're too sweet to be a deviant, sexual or otherwise."

Hysterical laughter bubbling within her, Lydia retorted, "I thought so, too. But evidently I am."

He looked at her thoughtfully. "Just what is it you wanted to try?"

Her cheeks hot, Lydia burrowed further against his chest, inhaling deeply of Shawn's cologne. Just his scent was enough to get her hot, it always had been. "I don't want to talk about it."

His hand left her hair and moved to her chin, cupping it and forcing her head up. Lydia struggled to meet his gaze, even as she wished he would just let the whole thing drop.

"Since when have we had secrets from each other?" he asked, shooting her a sad look.

"It's too embarrassing." Lydia imagined Shawn's gaze peering into her soul as he continued to just look at her. *If only he knew just what all I am keeping secret*, she thought.

Pulling away from his hand, she dipped her chin to her chest and sat up, bending her legs and wrapping her arms around them. "Since it's my birthday, he asked if I had anything I wanted to try. And I told him that I wanted him to dominate me."

"Pardon?" Shawn asked.

Lydia smiled sadly when Shawn's voice cracked as he spoke. "I didn't want him to hurt me, or anything like that. I just wanted him to, you know—dominant me. Tie me up, spank me, and maybe some light role-playing. I just wanted to feel helpless, completely at his mercy. And he did ask...."

Despite his having cleared his throat, Shawn's voice was still raspy when he spoke. "And was it just him you envisioned doing this? Or is it a fantasy of yours and you were willing to let him play the part?"

"Just let him I guess. He's not exactly the overpowering type. But I was willing to settle for him, if he'd at least consider it."

"But when you told him, he freaked, right?"

Lydia nodded, completely miserable. Now that he had forced her secret out of her, Shawn probably thought she was a freak too.

As his hand cupped her chin, she tried to resist, but he gently prevailed, forcing her gaze up to meet his. "He wasn't the right man for you, Lydia. He's not man enough for you. You intimidated him."

She couldn't believe it. Instead of pushing her away, he was trying to make her feel better. Maybe he didn't think she was such a freak.

"Look at you, a successful entrepreneur with your own advertising company, and you're just twenty-five. The only thing he ever started on his own was a lemonade stand in elementary school. And that failed miserably."

A giggle escaped before she could control it. In answer, Shawn's lips curved into a grin. "It's true. We got drunk one night and he told me all about it. Showed me pictures his mom took too. And that's another problem; he's a momma's boy. He probably needed *you* to dominate *him,* not hand the reins over to him."

Remembering all the times that she had had to take control, she nodded.

"Well, there you have it. What you need is a man who is

secure enough in his masculinity to be willing to let you dominate, and to fulfill your fantasies, including letting you submit to him. And I know the perfect guy for you."

"You do?" Afraid of which one of his friends he was going to try to set her up with, she almost didn't ask. She didn't want one of his friends. She wanted him.

"Yeah, I do." Without any warning, his head swooped down and his lips pressed against hers. Unconsciously, her lips parted beneath his, allowing his tongue entrance into her mouth. And that quickly, the suspense was over. "Me."

Lydia giggled again, hoping she hadn't heard him wrong; her ears were still ringing from that kiss. She was still afraid to act in case she had misunderstood it all.

"Let me prove it to you."

Still shocked, she just nodded.

"Run."

"Wha-at?"

"Get up off of my lap, and run. And when I catch you, I expect you to put up a fight."

On shaky legs, Lydia stood and moved around the couch. Like a deer caught in headlights, she remained there, waiting for him to move. His head whipped around, his gaze locking on her. She wasn't certain what she saw in his eyes, but it had never been there before. He looked almost—feral.

"I. Said. Run," he bit out and stood.

With a shriek, Lydia took off, running out of the living room, her bathrobe flaring around her hips. She turned the corner and paused, peeking her head back into the living room in time to see him leap off the couch and move across the room like a panther stalking his prey.

Her bare feet slapped against the hardwood stairs as she hurried up, Shawn hot on her heels. As she reached the top, she could hear his breath right behind her. He reached out a hand, and she barely managed to dart away, pushing into her office and slamming the door.

Shawn pounded on the door, then tried the knob. As the door swung open, he was wearing a triumphant grin. Lydia backed away from him as he crossed the room toward her. This wasn't the Shawn she knew, the calm and controlled gentleman.

Just as he was about to grab her, she ducked under his outstretched arm and raced away. Panting with her exertions and the thrill of being chased, she raced back down the stairs. Shawn pounded down behind her, and succeeded in tackling her at the base of the stairs. Even as she fell, she registered his body turning to cushion her fall.

Trapped against his chest, she wiggled, trying to get away. His strong hands clasped her around the waist, his legs locked around hers, holding her pinned. She went on wiggling, thrilled at the sensation of his hard cock digging into her back. Suddenly, she didn't have the will to struggle anymore. She was aroused, and she had a feeling that he was more than aware of it. If she had to bet on it, she would lay money on her panties being soaked by now.

"You done struggling now?" Shawn whispered in her ear, his breath tickling the sensitive lobe. In response, she renewed her struggles, but soon gave up. She was well and truly pinned. "Good girl. Now I'm going to let you go and you're going to walk slowly and sweetly up the stairs. If I have to chase you again, it won't go well for you." There was the briefest hint of steel to his voice, which caused Lydia's pulse to flutter. She wanted to protest that she had only made him chase her because he told her to, but this was what she had been dreaming of—Shawn bending her to his will. She couldn't have planned a better birthday if she had tried.

Nodding her head against his chest, she agreed to behave herself.

His arms and legs relaxed, allowing her to climb off him. As she stepped away, he rocked up onto his shoulders, pulled his feet up, and kicked out, thrusting himself upright. The fluidity of his movements, the sheer power, had her jaw dropping. She had seen him do some interesting moves like that back when they had worked out together and he had taught her to defend herself—which, coincidentally, was when she had discovered how much she liked being pinned down, by the right man.

But she didn't have time to drool as she would have liked because he moved toward her now, herding her backward. That look was back in his eyes, the one that screamed "dominant male."

As she turned and headed back up the stairs, she could feel him looming behind her, the heat of his skin radiating against her. She shivered at the image it evoked: his nude sweat-drenched body covering her as he held her wrists pinned in one hand, the other holding him up as he thrust into her.

When she reached the landing, she paused. Shawn leaned in, his breath hot and moist against her neck. "Having second thoughts?"

Lydia shook her head and forced a simple "No" past her parched lips. Licking them, she tried to vocalize her dilemma. "Do you want me to change? Or just, um, strip?"

"I want you to go into the bedroom, and then I'm going to do what I want to you, when I want. You'll wait, wondering what I want you to do next, what I will do to you next."

If Shawn's hand hadn't pressed gently against her back, Lydia wasn't sure she would have been able to move, the idea was so delicious. Helpless, completely bent to his will, his whims.

Shawn stopped her as she reached the bed and turned her around, pulling her into his arms. "I wanted to go slow," he growled, "to savor you this first time. But I've waited so long."

His mouth crashed down over hers, his tongue taking possession of her mouth. Lydia almost fainted at the sweet euphoria flooding through her. This was what she had always wanted, not the lukewarm passion she had settled for till now. As she submitted completely to his touch, she felt freer than she had ever dreamed she could.

Shawn cupped her ass, gently kneading the flesh as he pulled her tighter into his body. His legs bracketed hers, holding her tucked against the cradle of his body. He tore his lips from her.

"How I want you," he whispered, his voice trembling with emotions Lydia couldn't even begin to separate and define.

Stepping back, he twisted them around so that his back was to the bed. Slowly, he sat down, his hands retaining a firm grip on her hips. "Now, strip for me."

Shyly Lydia stepped back and raised her hands to her hair, pulling the tresses free from the clip holding them up. As the silken strands settled about her shoulders, she turned her back to him. Untying the belt of her robe, she quickly let it slide to the floor. Unbuttoning her pajama top, she let it dip slightly back, exposing the briefest hint of shoulders, before letting it slip completely to the floor, her breasts bared to the air-conditioned air circulating throughout the room.

She paused, uncertain. She could hear Shawn breathing harshly behind her, but even as she knew he wanted her, she wasn't certain just what to do. Having a fantasy was one thing—knowing how to carry it out was completely different.

"Turn around."

Lydia obeyed the command in his voice, her chin tucked against her chest. She could hear the bed creak as he stood. His fingers were firm and gentle as Shawn cupped her chin, forcing her gaze to his.

"Continue."

After loosening the tie of her pajama bottoms, she gave them a soft push, sliding them down her legs to pool at her feet. All that was left to remove was her panties, and then she would be bared to Shawn's knowing eyes. Her gaze still locked on his, she grabbed the ties at the sides of her thong and tugged, sending it floating to the floor.

As his eyes drifted over her, she trembled, knowing what he was seeing: the hard beads of her nipples begging to be touched, the faint tan lines of her bathing suit, her smooth-shaven pussy, her lips glistening with the beginnings of her desire. And all she could do was stand there while he was scanning her, taking her in.

Unable to stand the suspense, she closed her eyes. If anything, that made it worse. Now she was lost, wondering where he was looking, unable to see his eyes and know what he was thinking.

It was definitely the best, but most emotionally draining and oddly exhilarating birthday she had ever had. And from what Shawn had said, this was only the beginning.

Lydia jumped as his knuckles brushed against her neck, trailing down her shoulder to the upper curve of her breast. "He was a fool."

Opening her own eyes once more, she smiled at how dark and deep his appeared. His hand continued its path, trailing down her ribs to her waist, where it stopped. He applied the slightest pressure as he stepped back, drawing her to the bed, where he once more sat down.

"Come here," he said, patting his thighs. When she moved to straddle him, he shook his head. "No, lie across them."

He couldn't be asking what she thought. As she awkwardly lay down across his thighs he made no move to stop her, and she knew he did mean it. He was actually going to spank her.

But he didn't. Instead, his hand gently traced up and down her back and over the smooth curves of her ass. Lydia relaxed against him, soothed by his touch, even as a voice in the back of her mind screamed that she was bare-ass naked over a fully clothed man's lap—her best friend's lap at that.

Shawn's fingers started to dip and tease, no longer soothing, as he gently thrust into her core, massaging the tiny bud of her clit with his thumb.

Lydia twitched on his lap, her hands braced against the floor. She could feel the slick inner walls of her pussy clenching around his fingers, begging him silently for more.

"Like this?" he asked, his voice husky with need.

She moaned softly in answer.

"Good. How about this?" And that was all the warning she received before his palm landed with a solid *smack!*

She jerked, emitting a faint yelp. Fingers of fire spread through her ass, trailing directly to her clit. "Do you want more?"

"Yes," she panted, closing her eyes in anticipation. Shawn thrust his fingers deep, then landed another blow.

Lydia jerked under the sweet sting, raising her ass slightly for more, which he gave—three smacks in quick succession. Followed by his fingers doing things inside of her she couldn't describe but which caused her toes to curl.

"How old is the birthday girl today, twenty-five? Should she get a swat for each year?"

Her ass was already on fire, and he wanted to do twenty more? Oh god, she would die first. But what a way to go.

"Yes, please, Shawn." And he granted her wish, drawing each swat out as he played her body like a finely tuned instrument, tugging just hard enough on her clit to produce the most exquisite sensation, before doubling it with another hard spank.

She was sure she wouldn't be able to sit for a week, but she didn't care. His hot breath sounded harsh between the swats, a perfect match for her own panting gasps as she twisted on his lap, eager for more while at the same time she questioned whether or not she could take it.

"Please, Shawn," she panted. Her pussy was on fire, her ass stung and she wanted nothing more than to feel him driving into her, his hard cock claiming her in a millenniums-old ritual of male domination.

"Just one more, baby," he answered, "you can take it."

As his palm landed the final blow, he thrust a third finger into her core. Lydia screamed as sensations erupted through her body, pleasure blending with pain until she didn't know where one began and the other ended. She floated in the euphoria, completely pliant to his hands as he moved her from his lap to the bed.

She opened her eyes to find Shawn standing between her legs, his hands fisted at his side. His nostrils flared with each breath he took. Tormented need twisted his lips into a frown, and his eyes were closed.

"Shawn?" She hesitantly sat up, her hands reaching out to him. "Did I do something wrong?"

"God no!" he exploded as his eyes flew open. "I just want... but I don't want to hurt you."

"Hurt me?"

"I want to fuck you."

Lydia gasped at his crudeness. This wasn't the Shawn she was used to seeing, but it was the one she had always hoped for.

"I've been dreaming about it for weeks, fantasizing about laying you over my lap and spanking your rounded ass until you come, then slamming into you so hard your teeth rattle. But if I do, I'm going to hurt you, and you'll never let me be with you again."

"Shawn, you won't hurt me." But he didn't seem to be listening, lost in his own fears. Just as she had been when the fantasies of being dominated had started.

Relaxing back into the bed, she bent her knees and lifted her feet, pressing her heels against the curve of the mattress. Parting her legs as wide as they would go, she opened herself, even as she trembled. She felt completely exposed. Fisting her hands in the sheets, she waited. Her gaze locked with Shawn's, and she could see his struggle. Although her mind rebelled at what she was doing, her heart demanded she say it. "Master, please."

Shawn's eyes widened and he seemed to actually see her for the first time since she lay back.

"I need you."

Shawn's hands slid up her thighs, trembling as he caressed her. Lydia responded by widening the cradle of her thighs, offering herself to him. It was the ultimate submission, beyond any fantasy she had ever had, and she was willing to make it for Shawn. But only for him.

He widened his stance, his gaze meeting hers. "Are you sure?"

"As you wish Shawn. I'm yours."

His hands dropped to his waist and pulled his shirt free, tossing it over his shoulder. He unbuttoned his jeans and pulled then down his hips, but left them on. He gave a tug to the opening of his boxers, pulling the button completely off. Lydia trembled as his cock sprang free, as thick and hard as she had imagined it to be when she was lying over his lap.

"Put your arms over your head." The steel was back in this voice.

With one hand on his cock, Shawn lifted his other to hers, encircling her wrists, pinning them against the mattress as he restrained her, the fine matting of hair on his chest tickling her nipples.

Once more, his fingers did things to her, things she had never imagined, as they manipulated her clit and lips. She bucked against him, desperate for deeper contact, as he teased her with his cockhead, brushing it against her lips.

Just when she was about to cry out in frustration, he thrust hard, driving his cock deep within her. Lydia screamed at the sudden invasion, even as she wrapped her legs around his waist to hold him there. His hand moved from their joining, bracing on the bed.

She arched her back, pressing her breasts against his chest as he started to thrust, pounding into her willing flesh. He bit into her neck, marking her as his, and she loved it.

Shawn's sweat mingled with hers, coating them both, as he claimed her, driving them both closer to the edge.

Lydia's pussy ached, clenching him tightly as he withdrew, then tighter as he thrust back in. She lost track of time, enveloped in sensation. This was her fantasy fulfilled, and then some.

And then she thought *no more,* as with a savage thrust, Shawn pushed her into orgasm. Hoarse screams filled the room, and she dimly recognized them as her own, but couldn't and wouldn't make them stop.

It was only when his voice joined hers, shouting out his release before he collapsed on top of her, that she stopped. His hold on her wrists slackened, and she wrapped her arms around his neck, holding him pressed against her.

"Happy birthday, baby," Shawn whispered.

"Mmm," she murmured back, too sated to bother with words. Despite the awful beginning to the day, it was looking to be the best birthday yet.

THE BIRTHDAY TREAT

Jolene Hui

It was nearly birthday time again. This year I would turn thirty-four. Still single. Still trying to figure out what the hell life was all about.

The Wednesday before my birthday, I received a birthday package from my mom. It was wrapped in balloon paper with little turtles on the front. She had always called me "Turtle," because I had this stuffed animal I just couldn't break myself of. On top there was a note fastened: *Don't open this till your birthday...or else.* What? Did my mom think I was still five? I could wait until my birthday. It was only two days away and her gift was really the only thing I had to look forward to.

Jillian and I were scheduled to go out for drinks on Friday after work to celebrate the horrific occasion.

As I sat in my office on Thursday, I zoned out while squishing my earth stress ball repeatedly. I thought of the life I didn't have. The life that I had always wanted but had somehow escaped me: the large Victorian house, picket fence, dog, two kids, and handsome husband with a fabulous job. It apparently was not intended for me, as by now nearly all of my friends except for Jillian had husbands and beautiful children. The ringing phone interrupted my thoughts of bounding around on the beach with Fido, little Lizzie, little Joe, and my muscular man.

"This is Lynn, how can I help you?"

"One more day!" It was Jillian's squeaky voice.

"Why?" I put my head between my legs and sucked in my breath.

"Should I invite the crew?" Jillian asked.

"No!" I screamed, then breathed in a puff of air, my nose plugging and the blood filling my head. "I don't want anyone else there to celebrate my humiliation."

"Oh come on," said Jillian. "Bobby, Jim, and Susie really want to be there!"

"No, no, NO!" I shouted, sitting upright, the blood flowing back down correctly through the rest of my body. Good thing I had closed my office door.

"Well, you have no say in it. I'm picking you up at eight sharp. You better be dressed and ready."

"But..." I trailed off. Jillian had already hung up.

That night I went home and went through mounds and more mounds of clothing. I wasn't sure what exactly to wear the next day. Should I do flashy? Sexy?

I was on my fourth beer and modeling my fortieth outfit when midnight struck. I heard the chimes of my antique clock in the living room. My mom's gift was in the entryway. Since it was technically my birthday, I could finally open the gift.

On the front of the card was a picture of a little girl standing in front of a mirror in full dress-up regalia. Inside, my mom had scribbled, *I had hoped for grandchildren by now, but, oh well, Turtle, you might as well not deprive yourself of sexual pleasure.*

I tore open the wrapping and there it was—a slim, pink, slick mini-torpedo vibrator. My mom had gotten me a vibrator. She had given up on me. The packaging was pretty hilarious, depicting a wan-looking coed sitting in a field of daisies. Did she think this was really my first vibrator? My first vibrator had made its way into my bed when my boyfriend in college was so much of a drunk he regularly passed out before we could have sex. My first vibrator, which I named Steve, was my favorite sexual partner at that time in my life. Steve was slim, lime green, and always there when I needed him—especially after a long night of studying when I was stressed before a final, and even when I wanted to entertain guests that stumbled home with me after fraternity parties. If my mom thought I'd never used a vibrator, she was seriously kidding herself. But maybe she was just being clever. Maybe she just wanted me to feel youthful. I laughed and slipped the package into my handbag.

"Happy birthday, you hot piece of ass, you!" Jillian's voice buzzed into my living room at eight o'clock the following night. I was putting the finishing touches on my freshly done hairdo when I heard her echoing voice.

"Come on up, Jilly," I said into the intercom, rubbing some gloss across my lips and slipping my heels on. I grabbed my bag just as Jillian burst through the doorway.

"I am taking you out for a wonderful evening, my dear." In usual Jillian style, her hair was up in a French twist and she wore pearls around her neck and a sexy strapless dress on her slim body.

I always felt so much less sexy around Jillian. But tonight I didn't care. I was in a little black skirt and see-through top, my hair freshly straightened with a flattening iron I had treated myself to for my special day.

"We're going to Charlie's for tapas and wine and then we're going out to Turtle Island with the crew!" Jillian grabbed me and wrapped me in her thin, tanned arms. "I called them even though you told me not to!"

"Jilly, I don't know!" I pulled away and started heading out the door. "Have you ever even been to that club? And isn't Turtle Island a snorkeling island in Maui? I'll just get depressed that I'm not in Maui. I think this club is mostly a college crowd or something."

"Exactly," Jillian said as she shuffled behind me down the stairs. "That's just what you need."

"Happy birthday to you!" The staff at Charlie's sang loudly and banged their tambourines as a candle burned slowly in a slice of raspberry cheesecake.

As they walked away, I downed the rest of my Merlot and grabbed a fork. "God, Jilly, I am so damn old now, huh?"

"Old? Oh come on, babe, you look amazing tonight. Every guy who walks by stares at you."

We had just finished looking at my new toy and having a good laugh about the innocent-looking girl on the front. "They do not," I countered. "I look so old and haggish." The server came by and refilled my glass.

"Hey, slow down, hon, we still have to get to the club."

I took the last bite of my birthday cheesecake and started to sip the glass of wine. I could feel my face flushing from the alcohol I'd had already. And the wine was going straight to my groin. I could feel it pulsing. Maybe the club wouldn't be such a bad idea.

"I'll be right back," I said, standing up to head to the ladies' room.

When I stood up I felt a hand on my lower back. I turned around and came face to face with a young, tall, blond, hot guy in a silver shirt. I'd seen him earlier in the evening, but hadn't realized that he'd caught me looking.

"Hey, beautiful," he said, perfect white teeth glowing. "Happy birthday."

"Thanks," I stammered before starting to walk away. God, he was handsome.

"Wait a minute." Blondie began to follow me as I walked to the restroom.

The restaurant was crowded, and I thought I'd lost him as I made my way through the people, but when I came out, he was waiting for me. My thong dampened at the thought of his lips on my neck.

"Come outside with me for a smoke?" he asked and gently touched my elbow.

"But my friend is waiting for me at the bar…."

I felt a fingertip on my shoulder. It was Jillian.

"I've already paid up. I've gotta make a phone call and I'll meet you outside in ten, okay?" She winked and left me alone. Now my dream man and I were staring at each other. "Outside?" he asked again.

Without another word, I followed Blondie back through the restaurant to the rear door. He pulled out a pack and offered me one. It was my birthday so I accepted. I could smell his cologne as he made small talk with me. Everything he said was going right through my ears. I wasn't retaining anything because I was staring at his shiny silver shirt, sucking on a Camel, and fantasizing about what it would be like to fuck him.

"So, it's you're birthday. What are you, twenty-five?" He put his cigarette out on the ground.

"Sure, I'm twenty-five," I winked.

"How about I give you a birthday treat?"

A birthday treat. I liked the sound of that.

Before I knew what was happening, he stepped toward me and put his lips to mine. Although there were others outside, we didn't stop kissing. We were off in our own little area against the rear of the restaurant, and nobody seemed to be paying us much attention. As we kissed, we moved even further away from the few customers smoking nearby.

Blondie's hands worked expertly. He backed me up against the brick and slipped his hands under my sheer blouse, touching the front of my camisole. He pressed his body to mine. He was much taller than me so I could feel his hardness against my abdomen. My hands gravitated toward his crotch as if drawn by a magnet. I moaned as his hands went under my skirt.

"I was watching you," he said, his eyes bright.

"Yeah?" I murmured.

My handbag was still around my shoulder. An object pressed under my armpit and I pulled my hands from the hot zone to move it away. When I touched it, I realized what it was. It was my birthday gift. When I had taken it out of the package to show Jillian, I had inserted the batteries and even flipped the switch to make sure it worked. I pulled it out now and flipped the switch, glad that it was quiet, as we were just around the corner from the door.

"Oh, my," he whispered. "Look what we have here." His strong hand grabbed the slim buzzing object. When he flipped the switch to OFF and stuck it between his expert lips, I let out a breath and unzipped his pants. It was definitely my birthday, as an abundant present was waiting for me.

"Wait a second." Blondie took the vibrator out of his mouth and flipped the switch to ON. "You don't need to rush."

Putting the vibrator under my skirt, he moved my thong aside and eased the wet object inside my willing pussy. His tongue went to my mouth as his other hand slipped under my skirt to gently rub my clitoris. I started to thrust slightly against him and stroke his large silky cock. As he rubbed me, my feet started to shake in my high heels so I pushed back against the wall to help steady myself. The silk of his shirt rubbed against my cleavage. When I was on the verge of coming, Blondie flipped me around, my face against the brick wall. I felt the vibrator slip further up my cunt and his finger move from my clit to my anus. With the finger wet from my juice, he worked it slowly in and out, moistening me up. He added more spit, making me desperately wet back there, and I panted, my cheek up against the brick.

I couldn't believe we were going to do this—especially out here—but when I turned my head, I saw that we were all alone. Everyone else had gone back inside. My heart was pounding, but I realized that this was exactly what I desired.

"Say you want it," Blondie whispered, as if reading my mind.

"I want—"

"Say you want me to fuck you up the ass—"

Oh, Christ, I could hardly get the words out. Half-stuttering, I managed to whisper, "I want you—" a deep intake of breath "—I want you to fuck my ass."

He groaned at the sound of my voice, and when he finally slid his cock up my ass I was already coming, my come sticky on the birthday present in my cunt. I took the vibrator from him so he could put his hands on my hips to better work himself in and out. Every contour of his cock rubbed against the ridges of my asshole. When he came, he gripped my hips so hard I bit my lip to keep silent. I could feel the phone vibrating in the bag still hanging from my shoulder. He pulled his cock out and I reached into the bag to grab the cell. It was Jilly.

"Where are you, Jilly?" I asked, self-conscious about my breathing pattern.

"I'm still inside," she said. "I'm going to take a piss and I'll be right out."

"Okay, I'm still outside. I'll meet you out front in five."

"Everything okay?"

"Oh yeah, everything's good."

Blondie laughed when I said that. I hung up and turned around to see him running his hands through his sun-bleached hair. I put my phone and the toy in my bag and made sure that the vibrator wasn't sticking out where anyone could see it.

My skirt was a little crooked so I fixed it. When I looked up, Blondie was smiling at me. He kissed me quickly on the cheek. "Happy birthday, baby," he said before giving me a sexy wink and heading out into the parking lot.

"Oh my god, Lynn," Jillian said as we climbed into a cab. "That guy was so hot! Did you get his phone number?"

"Er, not exactly," I said, feeling his come dripping out onto the cab seat. "We just had a smoke and enjoyed each other's company."

"What, you mean you talked for a while and didn't even get his phone number or give him yours?" She looked shocked.

"Actually…" I trailed off and pulled out the shiny toy.

"Lynn!" Jillian exclaimed. "You naughty birthday girl! And you didn't even get his phone number?"

By the time we pulled up to the club I felt refreshed. My confidence had been boosted. I still had it in me even at thirty-four. The house, kids, and dog might have to wait, but at least, for a moment, I'd gotten the guy.

BIRTHDAY SPANKING

Mark Williams

Helena was known as one of the biggest bitches in our company, yet I found her charming, sexy, perhaps even lonely or confused. Certainly, she had an erratic personality. She could be sweet as all hell to me one week, then not even look at me or talk to me the next. Still, when she got really dressed up for work, which was about half the time, she looked damned hot.

The thing was, I could never tell how she was going to act toward me. Maybe that added to my interest in her. And I knew her birthday was approaching, which meant her behavior might become even more unpredictable. On the day itself, I took a chance and left a scarlet rose on her desk—anonymously. This threw her into a tizzy, as she couldn't imagine who could have done such a thing.

Finally, she glided over to my desk, dressed to the nines and looking spectacular. "Mikey, did you see anyone over by my desk earlier?"

"No," I answered honestly. "But the rose is from me."

She was startled and actually blushed. "Well, that was sweet of you. I never expected…"

"And I'd be happy to throw in a little birthday spanking, if you'd like," I whispered in my lowest possible voice.

"Excuse me?" she said, making me suddenly nervous. "Did I hear you correctly?"

"I hope so," I muttered.

"The only thing you're going to spank is your monkey, pal," she said in her bitchiest tone, before adding, "and I'm going to watch."

My cock hardened at once. I'm sure she knew it even though my lap was concealed by my desk. "Anything you say, Helena… just let me know when and where."

"How about right here, right now?"

My stomach tightened and my cock grew even harder. "This is a little too public, don't you think?" My desk was in an open area, making her suggestion far too risky to consider. At least, if we both wanted to still have jobs the following day.

She thought a second. "I suppose so. Follow me to the 'persons' room.' "

I did as ordered. Our unisex bathroom had a locking door. Perfect.

She went in first, and after looking around carefully, I followed. Without a word, she leaned forward on the bathroom sink, offering her skirt-covered ass to me.

"Do you still want to spank me?" she asked. I was too embarrassed to reply or move. I had never thought my joking remark would go this far, this fast. I was frozen until she said, "Go ahead, baby. It's okay." I moved behind her and raised her skirt as much as I could. Her slip moved easily with it. Her ass, now shielded only by panty hose, beckoned me. I raised my hand and gave her a playful but gentle slap.

"A little harder, Mike," she said, and moaned. I obeyed. She squirmed from the slap, but I couldn't help thinking she was enjoying herself as much as I was. I hit her several more times, each time a bit harder, then said, "Ummm...I don't honestly know how old you are."

"That's none of your fucking business. Give me one more hard one, and we'll call it even." I did just that, and she exhaled a loud groan. "Now it's your turn. I want you to spank yourself for me. Drop trou and do it, now!"

Given our location, there was urgency to the situation. I unbelted and unzipped my pants and let them fall to my ankles. I also pulled down my gray boxer briefs. My throbbing cock sprang to full attention once released.

"Oh, yeah," Helena smiled. "I never knew you were so big. Good for you, Mike. Now work your hand on it, like a good boy. *This* is gonna be my present."

I began to jerk off, needing no further incentive. Helena sat back on the sink and pulled up her long skirt in front, exposing her silky legs to help me further. I stood facing her, feeling foolish in my half-nakedness, but determined to come for her.

"Come on, Mike—" she murmured, encouraging me with her words.

I picked up my pace, feeling a tightening in my balls. Everything about the situation turned me on. Helena's stocking-clad thighs, the hungry look on her face, the way my hand still smarted from delivering her brief but thorough birthday bottom-warming.

"Are you close, baby?" She could see it in my face.

"Yes," I grimaced.

"Then start singing 'Happy Birthday' to me," she cooed.

I gave her a look of total disbelief, yet again I somehow managed to do as told. This was the strangest scene I'd ever been a part of. I knew that I'd never sing "Happy Birthday" the same way again, never even hear the song without thinking of Helena. My voice wavered as I did my best to sing the first line. "Happy birthday to you..." My balls tightened a bit more.

"Keep going, baby...."

"Happy birthday to you, happy birthday, dear Helena..." My body was in spasm. "Happy birthday to you!" I croaked. I was in full orgasm right now; warm, white come was everywhere. Helena slid off the sink and moved her mouth to my cock, licking and sucking up as much as she could.

"Now I've blown out my candle," she laughed.

I was weak everywhere. "God, Helena, you're so sexy...."

"I know," she grinned.

Slowly, I started to pull myself together while she watched.

"Since you've been such a good boy, Mike, maybe I'll plan a bigger surprise for *your* birthday," she promised, and I had a feeling she meant something a good deal more special than one solitary rose.

HIS
BIRTHDAY SUIT

Dante Davidson

Each year on October 2 Jack Mitchell bought a suit. He had an off-the-rack type of body: broad shoulders, hard flat waist, well-muscled chest. Simply put, he possessed a perfect figure for a size forty suit. In fact, he was basically an off-the-rack type of guy. He liked things simple; liked to know what to expect without a lot of hassle, without fucking around. Even though by now he could afford something a bit more exclusive, he found pleasure in walking through the same store each fall, choosing something fresh and new. After a careful look through the wares, he would locate his favorite, have any minor alterations made right then, and wear the suit out that very evening. This was his birthday tradition.

Although he preferred to think of himself as someone who favored routines, a nagging at the back of his mind made him think that he might be in a rut. Same store each year. Same way of celebrating his birthday. Even the same damn salesclerk, an elderly silver-haired gent with red suspenders stretched over a growing paunch, who'd been manning the store for as long as Jack had been alive. And on this October 2, that meant forty years.

So when he walked into Jones and Reynolds this year, he felt a wave of surprise at the appearance of the clerk he found behind the counter. She was slim and young, with glossy black hair combed backward toward the nape of her neck in an old-fashioned look, almost a modified pompadour. He did a double take, thinking he had accidentally walked into the wrong place, but no, there were the racks of suits, the crisp white dress shirts, the muted ties arrayed in fan shapes under the glass countertop.

Of course, the elderly owner had to take breaks sometimes. Jack understood that. Maybe he was on vacation. Or perhaps the man had even retired. But as he'd always been the one to help Jack with his purchases, he found himself at a loss for what to do. A wrench had been thrown into his intricate birthday plans.

"Help you?" the girl asked casually, and Jack realized that she had been reading a magazine in the dark gloom of the store. Curiosity made him wonder what she was reading, but he couldn't tell from where he stood. The place didn't have the best ambiance. It wasn't new, young, or hip. Yet he always returned here, rather than heading to a department store, because he appreciated the one-on-one service that made him feel like a real man, somehow. But he didn't think he'd be able to shop here now, not with this youngster watching him, or even—lord have mercy—*measuring* him.

He was ready to do an about-face, head out of the store and back to his car for a regrouping session, when she came around the counter. She had on dark-dyed stovepipe blue jeans rolled at the cuffs to reveal shiny patent leather boots with silver buckles adorning the ankles. On top, she was wearing what looked like one of the white men's button-down shirts that were for sale on the rack closest to Jack, along with a navy tie and an argyle sweater-vest in varying shades of blue—from cornflower to the color of a pale winter sky.

Jack looked at her a little harder. Was she trying to pass for a guy? Because, if so, she was doing a piss-poor job of it. No, she didn't have much in the chest department, but her eyes were ringed with a thick indigo pencil, and she had heavy mascara on her long, thick lashes. Her lips were a shade of red that made Jack think of the hard cherry candies his grandmother had kept in a crystal bowl on her coffee table.

"Help you?" the girl said again. "Sir?" she added, a little up-lift in her voice, as if working at acting the part of a shopgirl.

"I was looking for a suit," he said, not sure if he really meant it anymore, not sure if he felt like purchasing one after all. Why did he buy a new suit every year? Some crazy tradition that had started in his youth when he'd first had a little extra pocket change. A habit that he'd felt responsible for following. He bought a new suit every year. And Jack was a stickler for tradition.

"And you're about a forty, right?" She eyed him with her head tilted to one side, and he felt her thorough appraisal almost as if she'd placed her hands on him.

"Forty," he agreed. He was forty any way you cut it.

"For a special occasion?" she asked next, already scanning the wall behind him, probably mentally choosing suits for him to try on. Would she put him in a pinstripe? Or a double-breasted navy? He found that he was no longer so interested in the suits, but now that he had her attention, he also didn't feel like leaving. Where would he go, anyway? The morning of his birthday was always spent right here, in this store; had been for the past twenty years.

"My birthday," he said slowly. "It's my birthday—" He

looked down suddenly when he said it, embarrassed.

"Ah," she said, and when he finally looked over to meet her gaze, he saw that she was staring at him with a twinkle in her dark blue eyes. "A birthday suit."

In the dressing room, she pushed him up against the mirrored wall. She was slim, yes, but strong. Deceptively strong. She stood behind him in the mirror, and he could see suddenly that she had split her jeans open, to reveal what looked like a synthetic cock trapped in a cobalt blue harness. His eyes widened, and he felt as if his heart might stop. What had happened? How had he wound up here? When he'd poured his standard cup of extra-strong black coffee this morning, he'd imagined himself being fitted for a suit, not a strap-on.

But what was it he imagined at night, all alone in the center of his bed? Something very like this scene.

"Your birthday suit," she said, and she wasn't looking in the direction of the charcoal gray suit on the wooden hanger, but at him, her eyes indicating that he should strip. He couldn't believe the power in her gaze, like cold blue steel. How could she do this? Act this way, when she couldn't have been more than twenty-five?

"Now," she added, and he felt a shudder work through his entire body. It was clear to him that she meant business. And as he hadn't fled from the store at her first advance, she knew by now that he was interested. There was no denying, no hiding his desires. Quickly, he stripped out of his clothes, his gray cashmere V-neck sweater, white T-shirt, leather loafers, black socks, dark jeans. He stood, nervous, in his blue and white boxers, and she shook her head.

"I'm not going to be able to fuck you through those, am I?"

Closing his eyes for a moment, he wondered once more how

they'd gotten here so fast. To this point of no return. He'd never been even remotely close to this situation with a girlfriend before. Was that why none of his relationships had ever lasted long enough to see him through his birthday season? It wasn't his girlfriends' faults, he understood. They weren't to blame. He'd never been honest about his desires, never given in any further to his fantasies than making X-rated wishes over his birthday candles. Hadn't chosen the sort of girl who would feel comfortable packing a cock under her jeans.

"Come on, Jack," she insisted, and he felt another shudder work through him.

"How do you know me—?"

"I was waiting for you," she said, not waiting now, seemingly desperate to get to him, even though she was clearly in charge. She bent on her knees to slide his striped boxers down, watching fiercely as his thick erection sprang to immediate attention.

With a deep breath for nerves, he stepped out of the boxers, feeling more naked than he ever had felt before. More naked than when he changed at the locker room in the gym. Or when he'd skinny dipped that time in Hawaii. His handsome image was reflected into infinity, all angles visible in the three-way mirror of the roomy dressing room. And there she was, still in charge even on her knees, one hand on her own cock as if she fucked customers every day of the week, one hand on his. But she wasn't ready to fuck him. Not yet. Her cherry-slicked lips opened, and without waiting another second she drew in the head of his rod.

Jack leaned back against one mirrored wall, not feeling the cold glass behind him at all. The warmth of her mouth sent him into a bliss he could not remember experiencing till now. Sure, he'd had blow jobs before—good ones, too—but it was the knowledge of what was coming after that made this moment so damn hot. Her tongue swirled around his head magically, and Jack sighed harder and felt the muscles in his ass contract.

Between sucks and licks of his shaft, the girl started to talk to him. "You don't remember, I guess, but I was here a few years ago, helping out."

"Helping—" he stammered. Was that what she meant when she said she'd been waiting for him? Had she remembered that he came in every year?

Her mouth opened again, taking him in even further. She gave him a long, languorous lick before returning to her story.

"Family business, you know. Have to pay your dues," she said, and in a hazy state of mind, he thought back, remembered the blonde with the glasses and the book, never moving from behind the register. She'd been in yellow. Lemon yellow. And he'd thought how strange that color looked against the somber sea of suits. But that was some other girl. Younger. Plumper.

"Not—" he said, pressing back even harder against the mirror as she swirled her tongue around the head of his cock. Oh, fucking god, he was going to come right then if she let him, splatter against the mirror behind her, create a pattern of milky-whiteness on that polished silver surface. "She was—"

"Blonde," she grinned, licking her lips in a starkly wolfish manner before bobbing on his cock once more.

His mind wouldn't make sense of what she was saying. That girl had been different. He tried his best to focus his thoughts, but she continued the first-rate blow job, which made images burst randomly in his head. He inhaled deeply, realizing that he'd been holding his breath, and thought back to prior birthdays. The vision of the girl flickered through his mind once more. That other girl. What had she been reading? Something depressing as hell. Hubert Selby. *Last Exit to Brooklyn*. That was it. And she'd been eating candy, he remembered, eating hard candies as she read, cracking the candies between her teeth, then licking her fingers before turning the pages of her book. She'd seemed totally out of place in the store, and her father, no it must have been her grandfather, had apologized for her attitude.

"But—" he whispered, not able to make the link between that girl and this one.

"The bored blonde," she added, before sucking him so hard he could feel the pressure in the tips of his toes. Sucking him the way she'd sucked those candies, as if wanting to make him burst. He stopped trying to figure it all out for several seconds until she stood and put her hands on his hips and then spun him so he was facing one of the mirrors. "Palms flat," she told him. "Hold yourself steady."

"I don't—" He met her eyes in the mirror.

"Yeah, you do."

She reached into her pocket and pulled out a minibottle of lube, the type he'd noticed sometimes at drugstore checkouts, wondering who on earth would have the balls to buy them. Buying a pocket-sized bottle of lube was like admitting a dirty secret. He could imagine this girl buying them by the handful. She poured a half-dollar-size dollop into her palm and then jacked it against her own ever-ready shaft. He couldn't watch, but he also couldn't take his eyes off her. The blonde. The bored blonde. Transformed into this electric brunette, with the cold blue eyes and the icy smile. The blonde had been plump, he thought, and braced, with those large owlish glasses and the nose for reading.

She'd been at the counter for a few years and then disappeared, maybe for the last five birthdays. He had thought of her the first year she'd been gone, and not once since.

"Needed to get away," she explained as she set her body on

his. He could feel the cock against his ass, and he closed his eyes and lowered his head toward his chest. Shame floored him. How had she known? He'd never—

"Went to school back East. Lost the inhibitions, along with the braces, glasses, and a good twenty pounds. People walk on the East Coast."

"And you remember me?" He sounded nothing like his own voice.

"Look at me," she said, and he followed her order immediately, meeting her gaze in the mirror. "Course I remember you." Now her hands parted the cheeks of his hard ass so that the shaft of her toy pressed firmly against his hole. He tightened up, and she gave his asscheek a playful slap. "You were one of the only handsome guys to come in this place. We tend to cater to men who came of age in the middle of the last century. Guys who are the same age as my grandfather and his partner. But that's not why I remembered you—"

And now that cock was starting to slide inside, and he couldn't believe they were still talking, conversing, as if that plastic cock wasn't going to start ramming into him at any moment. Making him cream. Making all his birthday dreams come true.

"You were kind to me," she said, and now she slipped in a little further and he thought he might pass out at the pleasure. One of her hands snaked around his hip to grip on to his hard-on. He could feel her breath on the back of his neck, the softness of her argyle sweater-vest against his back, the crisp roughness of her jeans on his thighs. "You asked what I was reading. Nobody else did that. Nobody else ever seemed to even see me at all. So I looked you up. My grandfather keeps a shoe box of index cards on all his clients, and I saw that you came in on the same day each year. Made me curious."

As he was curious. As he'd always wondered what it would

be like to be fucked like this. The lube made the toy slide in easier, but she still took it slow. The head was painful, pushing forward, and then with an unexpected thrust, she was all the way inside of him, fucking him. And suddenly everything was a blur, the way she shifted her hips, thrusting forward; the way he could no longer force himself to meet her gaze. He had to close his eyes. The room was spinning, his thoughts were reeling. She jerked his cock for him as she fucked him, and he groaned, no more thoughts of anything. Just pleasure. Insane, fiery pleasure that worked through his whole body.

Nothing had ever felt like that.

He'd tried once before, with a toy he'd purchased on a whim for a girlfriend. He'd pressed the tip of it against his hole and frozen, unable to push it in, unable to give in to what he wanted. And even all by himself, he'd locked the bedroom door, had actually thrown away the dildo afterward, sick with his own ineffectiveness.

There was no denying it now. She knew. This girl knew. The way she manhandled him, touching him roughly, the way she talked to him. Nothing would be the same again.

When he came, it was as he'd imagined, splattering against the polished silver of the mirror, and then once more he was at a loss. What to do? Where to look? How to act? For the first time in his life, he had no tradition to follow. No habits to help him through the day.

She pulled out effortlessly and tucked her cock away, then spun him around once more and bent to lick the wetness from the tip of his cock. He shivered and ran his hands along the lean line of her neck, and she moaned for the first time, letting him know that she had received pleasure from his pleasure. With a sly smile, she leaned back against the far wall of the dressing room, watching him through those sapphire eyes.

"So I offered to take the shop today..."

Her head was tilted once more, admiring, appraising, as he fumbled to put his boxers back on, to get back into his jeans.

"I wanted to make sure that you had a happy birthday. And that it would go far beyond buying a brand-new suit." As she said the words, she eyed the single-breasted suit she'd chosen for him to try.

The suit on the hanger held no appeal for him now. But somehow he knew that, going forward, his birthday tradition would have a whole new meaning.

BIRTHDAY SPANKING, WITH A TWIST

Rachel Kramer Bussel

Although it is my birthday, I am in the mood to give my girl-friend my birthday spankings, and she is more than happy to comply. This routine—my beating her, my taking charge, my planning of just how things will go—feels like a perfect fit, like the turning of a lock over and over, until we've hit upon just the right combination. My birthday is but an excuse to extend our play even further, draw it out into an elaborate ritual to savor and cherish; to prolong her punishment in the guise of celebra-tion. I wake up seeing her tucked against me, curled into my body like an appendage; feeling like this will be the best day of the rest of my life.

I never thought that something as simple as the sound the flogger makes whizzing through the air, its purple lashes flying at breakneck speed before crashing down upon the thinly veiled bones of her back, could be so satisfying, but it is. She quickly awakens, peppers me with kisses and then, with a look of adoration, docilely turns over onto her stomach. I see her spine arching up at me; the small, rounded curves of her ass; her flowing blonde hair floating around her sides. The same as always, yet somehow more beautiful today, on a new bed, starting a new year. With Madonna doing it up, her English accent blaring out of the TV to cover the sound, I raise my arm and let it hit my girlfriend, hard, putting every bit of my morning energy into the strokes. I make her count, once for each year of my age, even though we hardly need an excuse, and watch as the suede strands, so simple, soft, and beautiful in slow motion, become something else when hurled with force. They twist and turn, become hard and solid, land with a thud so loud I feel the need to turn the sound up; my family is progressive, but not that progressive, and we don't want to overstay our exotic Los Angeles welcome.

The toy feels like an extension of myself, giving me the chance to give myself fully to her, to hold nothing back as I raise my arm as high as I can go, knowing that for her, it will never be too much. Her back is so thin, like the rest of her, that I wonder how she can take it, how exactly it feels as the strands slash against her upper back; though she moans as each red stripe appears across her backside, she arches up to take even more. I strike and strike and strike, making her count, all giggling gone as we move into another dimension. The birthday seems merely an excuse to do what we love best: transform ourselves from giddy, happy girls into another kind of person entirely.

I feel far removed from any dungeon scene, any false public notions of top and bottom. This is raw, as raw as I am making her skin now as it goes from pale to pink to red, as it takes and takes and takes way more than twenty-eight lashes. By around fifteen, we've both gone off to some other place, become slightly less than our individual selves as we meld into one continuous stream of motion. We stop counting once we reach my age, start counting other people's birthdays, stop pretending that we need some limit on what we can do to each other. Today there are no limits, only magic and trust, sorcery at the hands of a few bits of suede that mean more than a wedding ring ever could.

Later, when she fastens the collar I gave her only days before around her neck, which she always does voluntarily (I wouldn't want it any other way), I want to cry at the beauty of it. I've learned that some gifts are better to give than receive, and this is one of them, and in turn I've received the gift of being able to give myself to her. With every swing, every hit, every order, a little part of me enters her. It's a tempered wisdom, not so far from brute force that I can just let myself go. No, topping her requires the most supreme kind of control mixed with succumbing, putting my entire body and soul into each swing, yet never losing my mind. I keep us both with one part of ourselves on earth, letting the rest orbit, as we enter that magical place that helps sustain us through the rest of the daily grind. When I finally put the flogger aside and rub her back, now so covered in redness I have to search for the paleness beneath, the room is charged, heightened with the glow of energy we've created.

We go in the bathroom to brush our teeth and finish getting ready to go out for a special breakfast, and standing in front of the mirror, there it comes again, a wave of desire so huge I know I cannot resist it, despite my growling stomach. She looks so beautifully ordinary, so sweet and sexy as she vigorously brushes, fanatical about her dental care as only someone who professes to love dentist visits (and job interviews—no wonder she's a masochist) can be, and I have to have her again. Sometimes she is just too much for me, and I wonder if I can go a moment without touching her. I will have to later, but right now, I get her all to myself.

"Get down on the tiles," I tell her, knowing she has no idea what will happen next. For a moment, neither do I. I just want to see her on the ground, the way sometimes I just want to see her in the blindfold, or just want her to do something simply because I know she will do it, because I know I can have it. My simply speaking the words sparks something between us, solidifies the roles we've slid into so easily they feel innate. She has taught me that actions do often speak louder than words, and having a girl willing to do anything I ask is so incredibly sexy and powerful, like being granted my own personal genie. She lies down and closes her eyes and I push up her short skirt, the one she's just hastily pulled over her bony hips, and touch her pussy through her panties before tearing them away. I know the tile is cold on her ass but I know she doesn't care, will gladly do whatever I tell her to. She is bleeding but neither of us cares. In fact, I like it because it will help me get more of myself inside her.

I used to make lists months before my birthday, anxiously awaiting the given day to receive my numerous presents. I'd pore over each item on the list, gleefully anticipating the moment of arrival, until at some point that excitement tapered off, and birthdays somehow ceased to matter. Lists and parties felt too showy, too self-congratulatory; who really cared about a single day out of 365 that was only relevant to me, anyway? Gifts became incidental luxuries, not vital signs of birthday life. But somehow, like a real adult, she has managed to give me exactly what I want, something I could never put on a list—herself. With her eyes expertly glittering, her hair brushed and gleaming, all ready to go, we lie on the bathroom floor, with eyes only for each other. None of what we have to do today or what we will face outside of this room matters anymore. Now it is only about her hair splattered across the tile as she looks at me with awe and lust and obedience. I press the palm of my hand down on her clit, applying pressure anywhere I think will make a difference—anything to push her over that precious precipice. My other hand presses against her flat stomach, the one she always thinks is too big and I think is just right.

When she comes, her body silently shuddering, it's a gift that I'm well aware exists only in this moment, a once in a lifetime opportunity that I don't take lightly. I want to take full advantage of her, her body, her willingness, and my urge to plunder her that sometimes I don't even understand myself. But once I am there, once I am inside her, it all somehow makes perfect sense. This feels different than every other time, though I don't have time to analyze it. It's not something you can do a compare or contrast list for; instead it blankets you in a cocoon of want that transports you somewhere wholly unique.

"Nobody's ever touched me like this," she blurts out, clearly off somewhere else, somewhere magical I have taken her to. I know exactly what she means because I feel the same way as I push deeper, my hand slippery. I really slide inside her, eased by her blood and come and desire, the way she seems made for me to fit there, giving the lie to all who say that homosexuality is not the way our bodies were intended to be used. If that were the case, then this wouldn't feel so sacred, or be so simple, as if this is where my hand was always meant to be. She pushes back as I push in, a concerted, messy, glorious effort, and as I fuck her I can't help but think that she is the best and only birthday present I need. Maybe it's a sign of maturity, a gift granted that I hadn't even known I wanted; making someone else happy lifts me higher than any wrapped department store offering or lavish ornamentation ever could.

To be able to take her so high, both far away and right here in my arms, is the most special kind of blessing. I've also never felt anything quite like this. I want it to make perfect sense, I want there to be a logical explanation for why pushing my hand into her cunt makes my heart beat that much faster, makes my cunt twinge, makes my eyes fill up, makes my whole body get flushed and puffy with love. Is it because she is so eager to let me do whatever I want, trusting me to give her the pleasure she so clearly wants? Is it because doing so turns out to be so easy, easier with her than any other girl I've ever known, like I'm manipulating a windup toy set off by the simple press of a button? Is it because every time my fingers stroke that beautiful space between her legs, I feel like I am getting to see the real her—the one that's often hidden by her people-pleasing smiles, covered up in layers of color and powder; and her teasing with miniskirts and clingy shirts, doing everything she can to block others' views? Is it because it feels like her real self as she tightens around my hand, as she lets me go where no one has ever gone before, straight into her heart? Now, like this, with me, the only one she has to please is herself, and she does, forcing me to give her more and more, to push past any resistance she or I might have until we are nothing but raw muscle and sinew, fierce desire bottled into something so potent it could sweep us far away. She is not just giving herself to me, but grabbing, demanding, forcing me to fuck her with no trace of anything else but pure desire. For tearing me away from my garbled thoughts, for pulling me out of the nightmares that plague me, for plunging me, literally, into her, I am forever grateful to her.

I don't have time to stop and think in the moment, but later, I am filled with the pride of knowing I have done something I couldn't have done a year ago. She has made me into someone who can give her what she needs and appreciate the awe of her proffered backside, or front, every part of her a test and a challenge, a true gift. Some might say it's a selfish one, but I see how much she has to give up to let me hit her; to let me take over, invade her.

I don't know now that there won't be other birthdays with her like this one, that this is a one-shot deal, but even if I did know that, I wouldn't do anything differently. The day is sealed off, as if in a time capsule, a perfect bubble around it, as birthdays deserve.

All the rest that will come later I can forget, and instead of tears I will think of this room that we have consecrated with screams and smacks and blood and love. I'll think of my hand sliding inside her magic box and finding hidden treasure, her hair strewn across the floor, her eyes so deep and wide and open, like her cunt. I'll think of rolling over, pinning her down, squeezing that perfect ass as I ponder exactly how to administer that birthday spanking. Most of all, I'll remember waking up, that first dawning moment of recognition. I'll reach out, feel around for her, and there she'll be, the curve of her ass just as real in memory as on this most precious of birthdays, promising not only a wonderful day, but a wonderful year. This perfect moment is the one I want to stay in my mind, and hers, the one that will keep me young, inspire me during times when I have no one to lay across my lap except those who exist in my imagination, beckoning them forth out of the air, the city, wherever they are hiding, to come take their place amidst the candles and cupcakes of future birthdays. I'll be forever humbled by this memory, and forever wise, humbled and in awe at her ongoing gifts. I won't need another birthday to remind me.

YOU SAY IT'S YOUR BIRTHDAY

Alison Tyler

I didn't want to tell him it was my birthday. That particular confession seemed far too pathetic to say aloud. Here I was, out on a first date with a guy I'd just met a week before. A cute guy, with striking green eyes and longish black hair that curled when it met the top of his collar. He had on an eggplant-colored T-shirt that proclaimed I AM NOT A CROOK! and he wore his black leather wallet on a silver metal chain. Basically, West was cool—and I didn't want to admit that I was a total loser.

Let him find that out for himself.

What would he think if I told him that it was my birthday and that I'd had nowhere else to go, nobody else to see?

First birthday in a strange city. That's what it was. First birthday away from my controlling ex-boyfriend and my so-dull-you-could-jump-out-a-window-for-fun ex-hometown. I wondered what Don was doing tonight. Wondered *who* he was doing, to be truthful.

When I looked across the table at West, I realized that he was waiting for me to say something, and I understood I'd missed whatever question he'd just asked. Aside from my occasional spaciness, I thought that the date was going reasonably well. And even if I felt a nagging urge to confess due to my good-girl fixation, I kept the sensation to myself. I had no desire to spoil things. It had been six years since I'd been out on an actual date, and my instincts were rusty. Still, I was doing my best to be flirty and fascinating—and West didn't seem to sense anything strange at all.

"You look pretty tonight," he said as the waiter cleared our dinner plates. He said it as if he meant it, too. Not as a come-on. A statement. And I felt pleased by the clothes I'd chosen, a spangly silver tank dress, stack-heeled patent-leather Mary Janes, silver stockings. This was my birthday outfit, purchased at Nana on the Third Street Promenade, and even if I were the only one at the table who knew why I was so decked out for a casual dinner, I could tell from the expression on West's face that he approved.

We'd met in line at my new favorite coffee shop, and had experienced one of those instant connections that make your knees feel weak. Both of us ordered large black coffees, and we'd rolled our eyes at the fancy drinks being sipped around us—the nonfat, half-soy, double-shots with extra foam. When he'd asked for a date this night, I'd experienced a wave of nearly breathless relief. Having a date meant that I wasn't going to have to sit by myself on my brand-new sofa, surrounded by half-opened boxes and a half-empty bottle of wine. Or unopened boxes and a completely empty bottle of wine.

I had been saved.

"Tell me a secret," he said suddenly.

"A secret?"

We were at the dessert now, and I hesitated with a spoonful of cherry pie halfway to my lips.

"A secret," he said again, those green eyes flashing. "You know. Tell me more about yourself. Not just that you moved here for a new job. That you're still learning the highways. That you think everyone in L.A. looks spray-on tanned. But a real, honest-to-goodness, cross-your-heart-and-hope-to-die secret."

It's my birthday, I thought, but didn't say.

West stared at me, and I realized suddenly how good-looking he was. I'd been so sublimely focused on not being alone on this day, I hadn't really paid much attention to who I was not beng alone with. It was as if the actual flesh-and-blood person hadn't mattered. As if I needed just someone. Anyone. A fairy godfather. A Ken doll come to life. A birthday wish magically made true.

"You know," he teased. "A secret. The type you'd share with your best girlfriend. Over cosmos."

"I don't drink cosmos."

"Really?" his green eyes widened. "I thought all pretty girls in fancy high-heeled shoes drank cosmos."

I shook my head and when the waiter hesitated at our table to check on our drink status, I ordered a glass of my favorite whiskey.

"But that's not the secret," West insisted. "Because I would have learned that when the waiter came by anyway. You like the single malt, which is totally cool. But you still need to tell me something good. Something tasty."

"You do this on all your first dates?" I countered, buying myself time.

"I don't date that much," he said. "Been single for about a year. I wasn't really looking for a while. I've just been focused on work." He was editor-in-chief of a skateboarding magazine, which explained his hipster clothes and laid-back attitude. He couldn't have been more different than my ex-boyfriend, which was, of course, part of his appeal. "But back to you—"

My mind was reeling. *It's my birthday*, I thought again, but didn't say. "I'm a Capricorn," I told him. Here it was. A hint. A clue.

"That's your sign. Not a secret." He was grinning broadly now.

"I'm a natural blonde—"

"I would have found that out soon enough."

Now my eyebrows were raised. It was difficult for me to fathom that we had arrived here so quickly, at this place of coy sexual banter. But I started to sense that maybe I was going to have a bit of birthday sex. Another wish come true. The stars were aligned, as my friend Celia liked to say. Jupiter in my house. Or Mars up my skirt. Or something like that. "You're always this cocky?"

He shook his dark hair out of his eyes. "No. I just have a sense." His smile deepened.

"You have a sense that I'm easy—" His hand was on my thigh now under the table. I felt a shiver work through me. I liked the weight of his hand there, and I liked the fact that I knew it would slowly be working higher, inch by inch.

"No—that you're going to tell me a secret that's going to make me want to fuck you—"

God, there'd been no need to even tell him one of my secrets...that dirty talk is one of my ultimate turn-ons. He had guessed it on his own. I wondered what else he might sleuth out of me without me having to part my lips.

"I'll give you an example," he said softly, as his warm fingertips crested the top of my stockings to meet bare skin. "You wear garters and stockings rather than panty hose. You could have said *that*."

"But you would have found that out on your own," I whispered, echoing his own statement from moments before.

He shook his head, giving me a mock-sorrowful gaze. "How difficult is it to come up with one solitary secret to share with a stranger?"

When he put it that way, I realized that he was right. We'd talked in line at the coffee shop, chatted twice on the phone, but he knew almost nothing about me. He didn't know that my ex had cheated on me with one of my close friends, a girl I'd known since grammar school, or that I'd caught them in our bed when I'd come home early from work one day. He didn't know that I had left everyone I loved behind, in a mad flight to escape the pitying glances I seemed to meet on each street corner. He didn't know I'd dropped my engagement ring into a stream, watched the diamonds glint in the water, before heading for my plane. He didn't know that leaving Don had filled me with more relief than remorse.

And yet none of my past history seemed to matter now.

"Nica—" he prompted.

It's my birthday, I thought once more. *It's my birthday, and what I want more than anything is a delicious tryst between the sheets with a man who understands what I crave.*

Not that I had sheets. I'd put out a bedroll and a sleeping bag until I got my act together to buy a new bed and new bedding. For some reason, I'd believed a new birthday outfit was more important than a mattress. I'd told my best friend when I'd phoned her long distance. I'd said, "God, Celia. I'm alone on my thirtieth, and there's not one fucking thing I can do about it."

She had always been my savior. When I'd packed and moved, she'd been the only supportive member of my clan. When I was lonely in the night, she listened.

"You're fine," she told me.

"I'm about ready to call an escort service."

"Everything will work out. Trust me." Celia believed in signs. She believed in astrology and Good Moons rising. I listened politely, because we'd been friends so long. But I'd never given much weight to her astrological fixation. Yet she'd been right.

"Come on, Nica, tell me."

"Outside," I said, sounding as if I were begging for something, as he paid the tab. We walked out together, his arm around my waist and feeling natural there; when we reached his pickup, he kissed me. His lips were firm on mine. There was no question that he was in charge. I closed my eyes, feeling pleasure swirl over me.

"My place?" he asked, softly, "or yours?"

"I'm still unpacking," I told him. "The apartment's bare."

He drove to my new place anyway, watched me fumble with the key in the lock before taking it from me and opening the door himself. With what I was coming to think of as a familiar grin on his face, he watched me turn on the lights before turning them back off with a brush of his hand. The gold-red glow of Hollywood neon filled the room. Boxes were stacked all over, plastic wrap, crumpled papers, a phone sitting on one cardboard container.

"Your secret," he whispered, his mouth on my neck, not willing to drop this line of questioning.

I don't have any sheets, I thought.

I haven't slept with a new man in six years, I thought.

"It's my birthday," I heard myself say, the words finally breaking free, but too soft for him to hear. I cleared my throat and took a deep breath. "It's my birthday," I told him a little bit louder, then looked away. It was too dark to see his expression, anyway, but I didn't want to meet his eyes. Didn't want him to think I was such a sad case. Who goes out on a first date on her birthday?

Embarrassed, I was still looking away, as if deeply interested in a box in the corner, when I heard the sound of his belt buckle being undone. The quiet clink sent a fresh wave of anticipation through me. I turned quickly toward him, watching mesmerized as he pulled the belt free. Now my heart was pounding harder than ever.

"Your birthday," he said solemnly. "I'm honored."

Frozen, I stared as he stroked the well-worn brown leather strap between his elegant fingers.

"Honored?"

"To be the one to deliver your birthday spanking."

I could have melted right then. A pool of liquid sex. A glistening puddle reflecting the licorice red of the neon lights.

"I—" I stammered. "I mean, what—?"

"You know the drill," he said, his voice husky. "I can tell you do. Whether you've done this before in real life, or only in your fantasies. You know the drill."

And he was right. I did. But still I hesitated.

"Up against the wall," he said, sounding like an officer giving commands. "Lift your skirt to your waist, and then put your palms flat out in front of you."

I obeyed immediately, doing just what he said, hiking up my spangled hem, and then feeling West take over for me, holding my dress in place as he doubled up the belt and struck the first blow. He was working fast now, as if all that slow conversational foreplay in the restaurant had been a way to lead up to this.

The leather hit my panty-clad skin, and I sucked in my breath. God, how had he known? He struck me again, and a shudder worked through my entire body. The pain was sweet, stilling, and I focused on the bare white wall in front of my eyes as I counted silently to myself. The sting of the leather awakened an unexpected sensation inside me—the *old* me—the person I was before Don stamped all my desires away. The person I'd always longed to become again as I listened to Don snoring, while I stared out the window at the star-filled night sky and dreamed of neon instead.

West slapped my ass over and over with the folded leather of his belt, spanked me until I lowered my head and heard the keening of my breath through my teeth. I wondered if I should tell him how old I was, that it was my thirtieth birthday, that—

As if he sensed the whirring thoughts in my head, West put one hand on the side of my face and whispered, "Shhhh—"

I looked at him. Our eyes locked, and I felt as if he could see through me. See inside of me. He shook his head, as if that would somehow help me to become quiet inside, and then he said, "Don't worry so much," and it was as if a weight had lifted inside of me. Here I was, being punished by a stranger—he'd said it himself that we were strangers—and yet he seemed to know me. Know me better than my ex had after six years together. Know me better than I knew myself.

"Hold steady," he said, his voice low, "because this is going to hurt."

Oh, fuck, he *did* know me. He understood exactly what I needed.

"Sorry, baby," he continued, "but it *has* to. You know that. It has to—"

A chill ran through me, and I felt as if every sensation were electrified, as if the world had slowed down for the two of us. The noise of Hollywood disappeared. The nerves I'd felt all night vanished. West slapped the belt against my ass again, three more times in rapid succession, and then he said, "Step out of your panties."

The fact that he didn't take them off himself, that he made me strip for him while he watched, made me feel utterly ex-

posed. I fumbled, nervous, just as I had with the key in the door.
But this time, West didn't take over for me, he simply watched.
Finally, my fingers hot on the waistband of my little panties, I
got them past my garter belt and down my thighs, pulling them
all the way off and stepping away, leaving them in a silken ripple
on the floor. In a second, West was on me, not with the belt
this time, but with his body. I could hear the clink of his wallet
chain, feel the roughness of his slacks against my skin, feel his
whole body pressing me up against the wall.

He fucked me hard, fucked me until I was crying out, sand-
wiched between his body and the cool white plaster wall. I slid
one hand down my body, touching my pussy through my nearly
sheer dress. Adrenaline throbbed through me, and I rubbed two
fingers against my clit roughly, biting down on my bottom lip as
the climax built within me. West realized in an instant what I was
doing and pulled my hand away, replacing it with his own, sliding his fingers underneath my dress to touch my naked pussy.

I came when West came, our bodies working each other, taking everything we had to give.

Afterward we stayed like that, with West pressed hard against
me, until our breathing slowed back to normal. Until I could hear
the sounds of traffic once more, could see the neon glaze through
my wet eyes. West grabbed me up in his arms and then settled us
back down on the floor, with me cradled in his lap.

"I have a secret, too," West smiled at me, running one hand
through my hair to push the heavy blonde wave of it out of my
eyes. "I had an ulterior motive for asking you out tonight."

"Really—?" I asked, desperate to hear whatever he had to
say. "Really—?"

"I didn't want to spend it on my own either."

"No?" I murmured now, warm and safe in his strong embrace.

"You say it's your birthday," he said, and I knew in a flash what he was going to say a beat before he said it. The stars had aligned, like Celia had promised. I moved off his lap, and waited, in a crouch, hungry like an animal.

"It's *your* birthday, too—" I said before he could, and he nodded and handed over the belt and then stood and took his place against the wall.

ABOUT THE AUTHORS

RACHEL KRAMER BUSSEL is a prolific erotica writer, editor, and blogger. She serves as senior editor at *Penthouse Variations* and writes the "Lusty Lady" column for the *Village Voice*. Her books include *Naughty Spanking Stories from A to Z*, volumes 1 & 2; *First-Timers*; *Up All Night*; *Ultimate Undies*; *Sexiest Soles*; and *Glamour-Girls: Femme/Femme Erotica*, among others. The year 2007 sees the release of *He's on Top* and *She's on Top*, companion erotica anthologies dedicated to the thrill of dominance, and *Sex & Candy: Sugar Erotica*. Her writing has been published in over sixty anthologies, including *Best American Erotica 2004* and *2006*, as well as *AVN, Bust,* Cleansheets.com, *Diva, Girlfriends, Playgirl,* Mediabistro.com, *New York Post, San Francisco Chronicle, Punk Planet,* and *Zink*. She hosts In the Flesh Erotic Reading Series and gets off on watching people eat cupcakes, among many other fun activities. www.rachelkramerbussel.com

DANTE DAVIDSON is a tenured professor currently living on a sailboat in Santa Barbara, California. His erotic short stories have appeared in *Bondage*, the *Naughty Stories from A to Z* series, *Best Bondage Erotica*, and *Sweet Life*. With Alison Tyler, he is the coauthor of the best-selling collections of short fiction *Bondage on a Budget* and *Secrets for Great Sex After Fifty*.

ERICA DUMAS's short erotica has appeared in the *Sweet Life* series, the *Naughty Stories from A to Z* series, and numerous other anthologies. She lives with her lover in Southern California, where she is currently at work on a short-story collection and an erotic novel. She can be contacted at ericamdumas@yahoo.com.

SHANNA GERMAIN is a freelance writer based in Portland, OR. Her work has appeared in a wide variety of books, magazines, newspapers, and websites, including *Aqua Erotica*; *Best American Erotica 2007*; *Best Bondage Erotica 2*; *Luscious*; *Rode Hard, Put Away Wet*; and *Slave to Love*. When not writing erotica, she spends time teaching, traveling, and continually searching for that elusive grail, the perfect orgasm. You can read all about her online at www.shannagermain.com.

SIMONE HARLOW is a multipublished romance writer who lives in a small Southern California town where the houses outnumber the people. The former Catholic schoolgirl believes that one can never own too many red lipsticks, read too many books, or be too naughty. When not pounding away at the keyboard, Simone can be found with a tasty read, sipping martinis and watching the pool boy.

MICHAEL HEMMINGSON's most recent books are *The Yacht People*, *A Bed of Money*, and *Understanding William T. Vollmann*. He has sold a movie of the week to Lifetime and optioned a pilot to Fox.

MICHELLE HOUSTON has been writing erotica since 1995. She has had stories published in multiple anthologies, including *Heat Wave*; *Naughty Stories from A to Z*, volume 3; *Three-Way*; *Naughty Spanking Stories from A to Z*, volume 1; *Down & Dirty 2*; and *The Merry XXXmas Book of Erotica*. She also has several ebooks available from Renaissance E Books (www.renebooks.com). Read more about her or see more of her writings on her personal website The Erotic Pen (www.eroticpen.net). She loves to receive email at thewriter@eroticpen.net.

JOLENE HUI is a writer/actor who loves to watch TV, eat sweets, and dream of the day when she will get her Chinese Crested Hairless and Standard Poodle so that she can finally have the family she has always desired. She currently resides in Southern California with her writer/actor/musician boyfriend.

DEBRA HYDE's erotica has appeared in *Lips Like Sugar: Erotic Fantasies by Women*; *Slave to Love: Sexy Tales of Erotic Restraint*; and many other Cleis Press anthologies. Other recent credits include *Aqua Erotica 2: 12 Stories No Boundaries* and *Best Lesbian Erotica 2006*, with upcoming appearances in the *Fetish Chest* series and the second volume of *Naughty Spanking Stories from A to Z*. Her first novel, *Inequities*, is scheduled for late 2006. Please visit her long-running weblog, Pursed Lips, at www.pursedlips.com.

KATE LAURIE is an anthropology major who resides in beautiful Northern California with her husband and cat. She began writing fiction at an early age and switched her focus to erotica a few years ago. Her erotica stories have appeared in the anthology *Naked Erotica*, and on justusroux.com and satinslippers.com.

MARILYN JAYE LEWIS's erotic short stories and novellas have appeared in nearly fifty books and anthologies in the United States and Europe, and she has authored several erotic romance novels. She is the founder of the Erotic Authors Association and is the coeditor of the internationally best-selling art book *Mammoth Book of Erotic Photography*. Her erotic fiction has won many citations and awards, including the New Century Writers Award, and she was a finalist in the William Faulkner Writing Competition. Marilyn is the editor of a number of erotic short-story anthologies, including *Zowie! It's Yaoi: Western Girls Write Hot Stories of Boys' Love*. Upcoming novels include *Twilight of the Immortal*, *A Killing on Mercy Road*, and *Freak Parade*.

N. T. MORLEY is the author of more than a dozen published novels of dominance and submission, including *The Parlor*, *The Limousine*, *The Circle*, *The Nightclub*, *The Appointment*, and the trilogies *The Library*, *The Castle*, and *The Office*. Morley has also edited two anthologies, *MASTER* and *slave*.

EMILIE PARIS is a writer and editor. Her first novel, *Valentine*, is also available on audiotape from Passion Press. The audiotape version of her abridgment of the seventh-century novel, *The Carnal Prayer Mat*, won a *Publishers Weekly* Best Audio Award in the "Sexcapades" category. Her short stories have appeared in anthologies including *Naughty Stories from A to Z*, volumes 1 & 3; *Sweet Life*; volumes 1 & 2 and *Taboo*; and on the website www.goodvibes.com.

ABOUT THE EDITOR

Called "a trollop with a laptop" by *East Bay Express*, **ALISON TYLER** is naughty and she knows it. Over the past decade, Ms. Tyler has written more than twenty explicit novels, including *Learning to Love It, Strictly Confidential, Sweet Thing, Sticky Fingers* and *Something About Workmen* (all published by Black Lace), as well as *Rumors, Tiffany Twisted,* and *With or Without You* (Cheek). Her novels and short stories have been translated into Japanese, Dutch, German, Italian, Norwegian and Spanish. She is the editor of *Batteries Not Included* (Diva); *Heat Wave, Best Bondage Erotica* volumes 1 & 2, *The Merry XXXmas Book of Erotica, Luscious, Red Hot Erotica, The Happy Birthday Book of Erotica, Caught Looking* (with Rachel Kramer Bussel), *Slave to Love* and *Three-Way* (all from Cleis Press); *Naughty Fairy Tales from A to Z* (Plume); and the *Naughty Stories from A to Z* series, the *Down & Dirty* series, *Naked Erotica,* and *Juicy Erotica* (all from Pretty Things Press). Please visit www.prettythingspress.com.

Thirty-five is a very attractive age; London society is full of women who have of their own free choice remained thirty-five for years.

—Oscar Wilde